The Thirteenth Hour

The Thirteenth Hour

Laurel Rafferty

The Thirteenth Hour

First paperback edition published 2024
by Laurel Rafferty

The Thirteenth Hour is a work of fiction. Any resemblance to actual events, places, incidents, or persons, living or dead is entirely coincidental.

ISBN 978-1-0687373-0-5

Dedication

For my daughter Lauren.

The brightest and most beautiful star in my universe.

Chapter 1
Evergreen Care Home

Malcolm Banner pushes the empty wheelchair down the dimly lit corridor with one hand, while scratching his bum with the other. The wheelchair used to belong to Peggy in room number ten, but she's gone now. Part of his new job is clearing the elderly residents' rooms out after they've departed to what he hopes is a better world.

He's about to pass Audrey's room on the left, so braces himself for the acute smell of shit that will invade his nostrils and go on to permeate his maintenance coat for the rest of the day. *Why in God's name do they insist on leaving her door wide open?* Letting out a grunt, he inhales deeply and holds his breath whilst pushing past her room as fast as he can. The high-pitched squeaking coming from the wheels sounds like a mouse is being throttled.

Stopping outside the staff room, he pushes the wheelchair along the scuffed floor to the opposite wall where the others are kept. It twirls drunkenly, almost turning in a full circle before softly thumping into the rest of them. *Job done*. He's already thinking about how he can drag out having to do the morning rounds of sterilising all the commodes. He really can't bear the thought of it, not right before his lunchbreak. His old blue plastic gardening clogs are still splattered with brown remnants of yesterday's commode round — he needs new ones, but it will be a couple of weeks before he can afford them.

Malcolm's hopes for promotion can't come soon enough. Archie, the manager of The Evergreen Care Home reckons he's doing well in his new job, which is great as it means he's one step further to granting his mum's wish. According to Archie, Malcolm should be able to progress to personal care and become a companion for one of the residents. Post-pandemic, jobs in the industry seem to be hard to fill, so Malcolm thinks he's in with a good chance of a new role soon. Not only will he get a pay rise, but some other poor sod will be on commode duty.

Chewing his nails, he heads off towards the communal lounge which is his usual delay tactic. It's Monday and he's hoping they'll be playing the Elvis CD, which is his mum's favourite. Just hearing an Elvis track reminds him of why he's here. He usually takes a walk around the lounge, pretending he's looking for empty cups. The nurses don't seem to mind, judging by their impassive expressions. It probably gives them a break. He's in luck today, 'Return to Sender', his mums favourite track is playing in the background.

Malcolm never thought he'd find himself working as a carer for the elderly in his mid-forties. But given that he'd been looking after his mum since he could remember, it wasn't surprising. He'd left school at sixteen to look after her full time when she was diagnosed with Multiple Sclerosis. Her health had deteriorated quickly and he'd vowed to look after her ever since. He'd never known his dad, and caring for his mum alone during his adolescent years had left its scars. Even during his school days he'd found it hard to relate to his peers, never managing to forge any meaningful relationships with anyone apart from his mum and always feeling out of his depth in social situations.

Time had been sly and stolen Malcolm's youth along with his dreams of a successful future. The only thing he was any good at was fixing or creating things out of useless brick-a-brack. Probably from years of having to make do with whatever was lying around the house. It was hardly a skill that would make him a fortune. Money was always tight; they were just about keeping their heads above water.

Recently, his mum's health had got worse and social services started helping with her care, which meant Malcolm could finally get a job and although he's only been working for a few weeks, the extra money couldn't have come at a better time. Malcolm thought he'd hate work, but the care home isn't that bad and he's learning different duties every day.

It makes him feel like he's in a twilight zone, existing in a perpetual state of unreality, which suits his temperament as he doesn't have to think or talk too much to anyone about anything. Apart from cleaning the commodes and the constant smell of boiled cabbage and piss, he's quite happy with his new job.

As Malcolm exits the lounge, the main entrance doors bang open, bringing in an icy blast. Startled, he turns to see Dave, the Dial-a-Ride driver manhandling what can only be described as a human twiglet on legs through the double doors. Despite her frail-looking body she easily shakes her arm free of him. She turns to look directly at Malcolm, and as his beady eyes meet her translucent rheumy stare, his heart suddenly thumps in his chest, as if something has bolted straight through him. He stands gawping at her, rooted to the spot in shock.

She smiles, snake-like, at him. He lets out a small grunt. *God, some people are really creepy.* Recovering, he offers her a weak smile and a slight nod in welcome, then heads off whilst Dave escorts her to reception.

Chapter 2
Archie

'Mrs Clarissa Meyer, safely deposited!' Dave announces to Archie.

Archie is hunched forward, frowning at his open laptop. He's dressed in his usual grey suit and red tie. His bald head has a slight sheen to it under the fluorescent tube lighting and his small round glasses make him look like an overaged schoolboy.

'Great, I was just wondering where she'd got to. We were expecting you earlier, why the delay?' Archie says, looking up from his screen.

Dave shrugs his shoulders nonchalantly, 'She started babbling on and on to someone called Herbert at her front door, just as she was leaving. Calling out that she wouldn't be long; that they'd have a lovely celebration when she got back. It took me ages to get her onto the bus, then she started speaking in some weird language. Buggered if I know who she was talking to, cos no one else was there.'

'Who the hell is that? There's no mention of someone called Herbert on her file,' mutters Archie.

'No idea,' says Dave, turning to leave. 'You know what they're like at that age. Silly old bat. It could be her hamster for all we know. She does seem a bit weird though, and that house I collected her from... Well, let's just say it gave me the shivers.'

'Okay, thanks. Where've you left her?' asks Archie.

'I gave the heads up to Mandy; she's just taking her to her room now by the looks of it,' Dave replies.

Archie quickly checks through her notes again. Name: *Mrs Clarissa Meyer*. Address: *The Manse, Angel Road, Canehill, London, N99 9LX*. No family, no serious medical complaints. He tuts. He should have checked the details that came through from head office, but he's always running behind with the paperwork. The file notes should provide more detailed information, such as Clarissa's full health history, next of kin details, and her likes and dislikes, but there's barely anything else other than her booking for a week's break with a companion, paying for one of their exclusive rooms overlooking the gardens. *She must be loaded*. Standing, he straightens his tie then makes his way down the corridor to welcome their new resident.

The door to room seven is wide open, and he can hear Mandy, one of the carers, going through mealtimes with Clarissa in an overly loud voice. Inside, Clarissa is sitting in an armchair, staring somewhere beyond Mandy's shoulder.

Archie coughs, announcing himself in the doorway.

Mandy looks up at him, appearing relieved.

'Oh, here he is now!' Mandy shouts. 'This is Archie, Clarissa! He'll have a little chat with you, make sure you're all settled. When he's finished, I'll take you to the dining room for a lovely bit of lunch. You can meet some of our other residents. It's Chef's special today — pork chops! Do you like pork chops, Clarissa?'

Mandy doesn't wait for an answer. She gives Archie a nervous smile, then hurries from the room.

Archie clocks her nervousness but reminds himself she's quite new to the job. Keen, but a way to go yet. He strides across the room, hand outstretched in welcome with a well-practised smile plastered on his face.

As Clarissa places her small bony hand in his and their eyes meet, he feels like he's been punched deep inside his solar plexus. He gasps. Stiffens. Blinks, then blinks again. For a split second, when their eyes met, it looked as though hers were glowing pure white. *Jesus!* he almost says aloud but realises it must have been a trick of the light as her dull watery eyes now look up at him. With a quick shake of his head, he clears his throat.

'Hello Clarissa. My name is Archie Barrington. Welcome to The Evergreen Care Home. I hope you enjoy your stay with us over the next week. So, you're here for some TLC, eh? Well, I can assure you, you've come to the right place. We've got lots of things lined up for you, including bingo! Do you like bingo, Clarissa?'

Clarissa looks at him with a strange, unreadable expression on her face. 'Oh, that sounds lovely,' she replies. 'When will my companion be joining me?'

Chapter 3
A Peculiar Pair

'Please turn that rubbish off dear, you know those ridiculous people on that show don't have a clue what they're talking about, they know absolutely nothing about real antiques! Now why don't you come and sit down and tell me a little bit more about yourself.' Clarissa says to Malcolm.

Sighing, Malcolm plonks himself down on the chair opposite Clarissa and switches the TV off with the remote. He was enjoying listening to the TV show whilst he was sorting through her laundry. The show was about people finding all sorts of treasures and antiques in their attics, some made a pretty penny. But it had been the same every day since he'd been her companion, he'd start doing the jobs that needed doing like her laundry or cleaning her room and all the while instead of watching the TV or reading a book or magazine, she'd just sit and watch him, muttering away to herself in a foreign language. At first he found it off putting, a bit weird even but other than that she seems harmless enough. It reminded him a little of his mum, she'd watch him when he was fixing things at home and they'd chat about whatever was on the telly or in the news. Whereas Clarissa seemed intent on grilling him, still she hadn't had children as far as he knew, so maybe she was just curious about his life.

'So, Malcolm, you said you had no family, did your parents die then?

'Um, yeah… well I don't know about my dad, cos like he ran off before I was born but my mum, well yeah, she's um… not here, he said turning scarlet at the lie.

'What about brothers and sisters?'

'Nah, there's just me and my mum… before she died, I mean.'

'I see, and do you have a girlfriend Malcolm?'

'Um, no.'

Perfect Clarissa thinks as she smiles sweetly at him.

Chapter 4
The Offer

It's Friday afternoon and Archie is feeling the effects of a busy week. He's climbing the stairs to the second floor, looking for Malcolm. As he reaches the top, huffing and puffing, he checks the corridor both ways. There's no sign of him. He should be on commode duty up here. *Where the hell is he?* As Archie peers into each of the rooms, his mind flips back to Clarissa. Just thinking about her troubles him. Each interaction he's had with her has made him feel uncomfortable for hours afterwards. She's been staying with them for a week now and he still dreads looking at her. *There's something about her — she seems so... what's the word he's looking for?*

'Ah! There you are, Malcom,' he calls breathlessly.

Malcolm emerges from room eleven with a disgusted look on his face. His arm is outstretched, clutching a commode in a blue gloved hand, pinching his nostrils shut with the other.

'When you've finished that, can you come to my office please? I need a word with you,' Archie says, trying to muster an encouraging smile but failing.

'Course, boss, soon as I've finished this,' Malcolm replies, looking anxious.

A few minutes later, as Archie sips his afternoon tea, he casts his mind back to Monday when Clarissa had arrived at Evergreen. He'd arranged for each of his carers to spend an hour or so with her so she could choose who she wanted as her companion. She'd made it quite clear, however, that none of them matched her expectations. That was until Malcolm had been sent to try and fix her bedroom window, which had got stuck. Clarissa had promptly informed Archie that Malcolm was the companion she wanted — but for the life of him, Archie can't understand why. Malcolm is okay at his job; he barely speaks or engages with anyone, and his social skills are minimal at best, but at the end of the day he is employed as a basic carer, and great social skills aren't strictly necessary.

As Malcolm bumbles into the office, sweating profusely, Archie tries not to breathe in too deeply as Malcolm's body odour invades the space between them. It seems to have reached new depths today. He waits patiently as Malcolm tries to compose himself, wiggling and jiggling in his seat, before finally offering Archie an apprehensive smile.

Archie peers curiously at Malcolm over the top of his glasses.

'So, Malcolm, you've been Clarissa's companion for nearly a week now. I know you've been busy, as you've had other duties as well, but how would you say you're getting on?'

Malcolm looks startled, as if this is some sort of test. 'Er yeah, no problem,' he says. 'She's er… okay when you, um… get to know her. She's a bit strange sometimes, like, but I don't mind that.'

Archie looks intently at Malcolm. 'What do you mean by strange?'

Malcolm seems to immediately regret his words and tries to backtrack, stuttering. 'Er sorry... it's just that she mutters in a strange language sometimes, when she's looking at me, and I'm not sure what she's saying, but that's okay — I don't mind.' He lets out a small nervous laugh.

Archie nods as if he's satisfied. 'Yes, I know what you mean, but apart from that would you say you're enjoying it?'

Malcolm straightens his back. 'Well, apart from all that — yes, it's... um — yes, okay. I think she's pleased with me,' he says, puffing out his chest slightly with pride. 'I even manged to sort out her dicky tummy… er, I mean her upset stomach.'

Archie drums his fingers on the desk, deep in thought. He nods and looks straight at

Malcolm as if he's made his mind up about something.

Malcolm appears to brace himself.

'As you know,' Archie continues, 'Clarissa is leaving here this afternoon. She's requested a companion for another week at her home address — starting from today — which will include being there this weekend.'

Archie looks intensely at Malcolm, gauging his reaction.

Malcolm stares blankly back.

Archie clears his throat, looking Malcolm in the eye. 'The thing is, Malcolm… Clarissa has asked if that companion could be you. Would you like to be her home companion for the next week?'

Malcolm's eyes widen. He nods dumbly. 'Er really? Well… yes… of course.

'Clarissa has offered a very generous amount of money,' Archie says. 'In fact, she's willing to pay you two thousand and… um sorry, I mean two thousand pounds for the week.'

'Oh my God!' exclaims Malcolm.

All that extra money. Malcolm flicks his eyes around the room, doing a quick calculation in his head — *that's more than I earn in a month!* He can't believe it. A smile suddenly splits his face, revealing his crooked teeth, but he doesn't care — all he can think about is the money. He tries not to start chewing his nails as he feels butterflies start to flutter about in his stomach.

He deserves this break. It's what he's been waiting for — a well-paid companion role, and best of all, he'll get the money he needs for his mum. He knows it'll mean leaving her for a week and he hates the thought of it, but the extra money will more than make up for it. He hadn't expected his mums health to go downhill so quickly, and if he doesn't find the cash to put his plan into action very soon, he may never get the chance to fulfil her last wish.

Malcolm nods excitedly. 'Um, yes, definitely... I can do that.'

'You're absolutely sure?' Archie checks. 'You don't mind going to live-in at her home address for the week? I'll understand if you can't. She wants someone from this evening, can you do it at such short notice?'

'Yeah, I can start tonight, if that's what she's asked for.' Malcolm is still dumbfounded about the two thousand pounds he'll get for just one week's work. He can't quite believe his good fortune and thinks it may lead to a permanent job. *Jesus, for that amount of pay — I'd even clean her commode.*

'Okay,' Archie says, somewhat apprehensively, 'Clarissa will be leaving soon, and she's asked that you arrive at her home address promptly to prepare her evening meal tonight. She's already written out the cheque for you.' Archie hands Malcolm a brown envelope.

'We'll expect you back here a week on Monday then.'

With trembling hands, Malcolm takes the envelope. As Malcolm leaves the office, Archie pats the five hundred pounds commission he was given by Clarissa which is now tucked in his breast pocket. *Very nice*, he thinks, congratulating himself. Still, something doesn't sit right with him. He feels uneasy but doesn't know why. At first glance, Clarissa Meyer looks like any other octogenarian, but every time she looks at him, he feels like she can see right inside him. No, it's not that, but whatever it is, it sends shivers down his spine and leaves him feeling cold.

Archie prints out a copy of the new staff rota and pins it to the notice board in the staff room, having taken Malcolm off of it for the following week. He'd allowed him to go home early to pack a bag and get the train to Clarissa's in time for her dinner. He'd had to give him clear written instructions on how to get to there as Malcolm's phone was so old it didn't have any modern apps on it.

On the books, it will look like Malcolm is away for the week. Archie had told Malcolm not to tell any other member of staff where he was going, as they would quite rightly wonder why he'd been chosen to do a companion's role. 'Shit! That reminds me,' he mutters, making a mental note to chase up Malcolm's references. He isn't even sure he has all Malcolm's personal details on file. Head Office would go mad if they knew. *Still,* he thinks, *they probably think it's easy having to do almost everything yourself in this bloody place — including trying to recruit carers for minimum wage.*

Chapter 5
Home Again

Clarissa is glad to be back at The Manse. She absolutely hates these yearly trips she has to undertake, but it allows them to have their annual celebration. Herbert used to go but he'd never get away with it now, he hasn't got a clue how things work in 2024.

Creeping into their master bedroom, she opens the drapes on their four-poster bed, pulling back the black sheet. She tenderly caresses the slumbering form that lays before her — her beloved Herbert. His beautiful silver eyes open; he gives her a rictus grin, revealing his shiny black pointed teeth. Her eyes move down his body with longing. He's still over six and a half feet tall. His long body appears willowy now, but his limbs are lithe and supernaturally strong, and even though he's growing weaker by the day, he can still move at lightning speed when he chooses. The love she feels for him has grown over a long lifetime. She'd been a young girl living in Hungary when

Herbert had first taken her, and with each passing celebration, their love only grows stronger.

Speaking in her native Hungarian tongue, Clarissa relays to Herbert the details of the agonising week-long stay she had to endure at The Evergreen Care Home. 'He's got no family to speak of, and no brains either. He's possibly the stupidest one we've ever had. No one will miss him — he's perfect. We may have to deal with some questions from that idiot manager and possibly the driver, because he never stopped staring at me during the whole way home. He gave me the creeps! We simply must remember to use private transport next time,' she says, stroking Herbert's face and kissing him tenderly on the forehead. 'Now my darling,' she says, rising, 'I must go and prepare. I want to make sure our new house guest has a warm welcome. After all, if it weren't for him, we couldn't have our special celebration. I'm sure once he knows what's expected of him, he'll love every minute of it!' Clarissa beams down at Herbert. 'And after last year's disaster, we don't want to make the same mistake again, now do we?'

Herbert emits a low keening sound in response. He always gets agitated just before a celebration and tonight is no different; he's restless and needs to eat.

'Don't worry my darling,' Clarissa croons soothingly. 'Not much longer now.'

Chapter 6
The Journey

Malcolm is still in shock. In fact, he's so dumbfounded he nearly forgets to deposit his cheque at the bank on his way to the underground station.

Canehill is just three stops south of the River Thames. He's never been to this part of London before. On the tube, he can't see where he's going, but to be honest, he doesn't care. All he wants is the money. If he makes a good impression, this could well be the break he's been waiting for. He's on his way to better things; he can feel it in his bones, and the best part is, his mum will get to see her brother, a wish neither of them thought possible. He's so busy daydreaming about everything, he almost misses his stop.

The high-pitched beeping of the doors opening brings Malcolm out of his reverie. Jumping up, he accidentally kicks the contents of his bag across the floor. Cursing, he just manages to clumsily stuff them back in and hurl himself through the doors before they snap shut on him.

On the street outside the tube station, he searches through his pockets for Archie's instructions. He finds them scrunched up in his back pocket. After scrutinising them, he heads off, wondering what the house might be like. He realises he doesn't know what a *Manse* is. He decides it's probably something fancy like a studio.

While he was her companion at Evergreen, all Clarissa ever talked about was bloody history, and it wasn't even the type of history he knew anything about. She ranted on and on about castles and masters of the old arts and how great the old world was. All he had wanted was for her to stop jabbering on and fall asleep so he could watch the TV in peace. And love! How she'd droned on and on about true love. 'It should be everlasting,' she'd said. Adding that '*mere mortals*' knew nothing of it.

As he turns on to Angel Road, thinking about how big the TV in his room might be, it dawns on him that The Manse doesn't have a house number. He peers more closely at the door numbers, which ascend on the side of the road he's walking along. Just then, an elderly woman appears at the front door nearest to him. She looks suspiciously at him then proceeds to stomp down the path, pushing a tartan shopping bag on wheels as if it were a weapon of mass destruction and she's charging into battle. Malcolm is standing in front of her gate and the woman looks affronted, prompting Malcolm to shuffle aside awkwardly.

The woman opens her gate and stands glaring at him.

Not able to make direct eye contact, Malcolm stutters, 'Um, excuse me. Madam? Miss? I wonder if you know where The Manse is? It says here... see? *The Manse, Angel Road.*'

Malcolm thrusts the bit of paper at her, his podgy hand trembling slightly.

She doesn't respond, so he continues hesitantly, 'But it don't have a number on it... and I'm, er... I'm not sure what it is.' Malcolm's voice trails off as he notices the woman's body stiffen and her eyes bulge.

The woman looks at the piece of crumpled paper as if it were a rattle snake and begins to back away.

In a tight, shrill voice that reminds Malcolm of his old headmistress, she trills, 'Continue straight up the road. When you reach the last house on this side, you'll see a big black gate. That's The Manse.' She makes it sound like an order. Then takes off down the road like a geriatric hare.

Malcolm grunts as he stares after her. Turning, he starts to walk up the road, thinking his old Mum was right: there are some very odd people about these days. As he trudges on, he thinks back to the message he left at home for her. He knows she'll be anxious whilst he's away.

He'd explained that he'd been offered a lot of money for doing a week's work for an elderly lady. He hated the thought of leaving her and worried about her being able to cope alone at night, although he knew the carer would make sure she got to bed alright. He had no choice though; he had made her a promise and he was determined to get the money they needed to carry out her wish.

Chapter 7
The Message

Archie dives into his office to take a breather. There are yellow sticky notes strewn across his desk. Glancing at them, he sees head office has called a couple of times, the chef is still moaning about the fridge not working properly, and one of the cleaners has come down with the flu. He can see others, but decides he'll check them after he's had his cuppa. Opening his laptop, he sees there are numerous emails marked urgent.

Just then, there's a slight tap on his office door. It's Mandy bringing him his tea.

'Here you go, Archie. Would you like some biscuits?'

Archie smiles. 'No thanks, but have you got a minute? I just want to ask you something about one of our residents.'

'Course, which one?' Mandy plonks herself down in the seat opposite Archie and raises her eyebrows in expectation.

Archie loosens his tie, feeling hot and uncomfortable. 'You remember Clarissa Meyer, the lady who stayed with us this week?'

'Oh her. Yes, she was a strange one.' Mandy looks up at Archie and blushes. 'Sorry! I didn't mean to be rude about her. It's just... I don't know, she seemed a bit weird if you know what I mean. She made me feel on edge. And it wasn't just me. In fact, I don't think anyone liked her. She didn't help herself either, even when she was supposed to be taking part in the group activities, she just stared at people without saying a word. It was very...' Mandy shakes her head, as if searching for the right word, 'off putting,' she blurts, laughing awkwardly. 'God, that sounds so silly now when I say it out loud.' She looks over at Archie as if to gauge his reaction. 'Sorry,' she gushes, 'I don't want to sound unkind. I hope you don't think I'm mad or anything, it's just....' she trails off.

'It's okay,' Archie cuts in, smiling. 'I appreciate your honesty, and yes, some of our residents can certainly appear a bit weird. Thankfully they're not all like that. But was there anything else you noticed about her?'

'No, not really. I know she didn't get on with the food very well, she barely touched it, but we didn't dare tell Chef, he'd have thrown a hissy fit — you know what he's like. Malcolm said she didn't complain about it, but what didn't help was when she had some of Vera's birthday cake and then threw up in the lounge. Malcolm had to take her to her room and give her something to settle her stomach. Other than that, no, nothing I can think of. I thought he was a real trooper for being her companion for a whole week. To be honest, I don't think I could have done it.'

'Okay Mandy, thanks — that's all for now.'

As Mandy gets up to leave, she looks back and says, 'Oh! That reminds me, I took a message from a Mrs Bonner? Or it might have been Mrs Banner? Anyway, it was something to do with Malcolm I think, but I couldn't understand her too well. I left her number on your desk.'

'Thanks,' replies Archie, frowning.

Archie rifles through all the sticky notes, wondering what the message could be about. Banner was Malcolm's surname. He finds the note, but all that's written on it is the name, '*Mrs Bonner/Banner?*' and a local number. Then, *Re: Malcolm?* He calls the number from his desk phone and lets it ring for a while. No answer. He'll try again later. As far as he knows, Malcolm isn't married, so he's not sure who it could be. He hopes to God it isn't some sort of family emergency. That would be a bloody disaster, because if Malcolm has to come back to sort it out, he'll have to pay back the commission money to Clarissa. He knows no one else would want to take over as Clarissa's companion, not even for a week. Swearing to himself under his breath, he decides he'll ring again after he's checked Malcolm's personal file. As he gets up to fetch the file, his desk phone starts ringing, he can see from the display that it's Chef calling from the kitchen, *what now? another emergency no doubt.* He doesn't bother answering, instead he makes his way to the kitchen, thinking he'll check Malcolm's file later.

Chapter 8
The Manse

It starts raining as Malcolm stands peering through the gothic iron gates at The Manse. He's never been to a house this big before. Gazing at the many windows for any signs of life, his stomach starts to get butterflies. The house is posh, he supposes, but he's slightly disappointed. It looks ancient, much older than the houses on the rest of the road. The garden is overgrown, with ivy claiming most of the exterior walls. The paint is peeling off in patches where the ivy isn't clinging to, as if the house is shedding its own skin.

There's an old-fashioned bell on a rope attached to the gate. He gives himself a quick once over, pulling and stretching his jumper down to cover his ever-expanding belly, and running his hand through his dark, greasy hair. He sees now that his shoes are badly scuffed; he didn't have time to polish them. *Too late now*, he thinks as he takes a deep breath and pulls the rope.

The rusted iron gates open slowly. Screeching in protest, they seem to take an age to open fully. As soon as they do, Malcolm meanders up the gravel path towards the large front door, noticing all the shrubbery on either side of the path is dead. The front door is ajar, but he can't see beyond it — only darkness. There are no lights and no sign of the person who left the door open. It's grown dark over the last hour and the dim streetlamp on the main road behind him does little to light the way.

As the rain lashes down, he tries to peer beyond the door into the house, but the rain is in his eyes and he doesn't see the dip in the path. He stumbles, only just managing to steady himself before almost hurtling headfirst into the gravel. Righting himself, he grunts and looks up. Clarissa is standing in the open doorway, staring straight at him, soft light now glowing from behind her. Startled, he just gawps at her. How did she just appear like that? *And God, what on earth is she wearing?* He can't quite make out the details of her face, but she's wearing a long black gown and her hair is no longer billowing above her head like a puffy white cloud of candyfloss but is trailing loosely around her shoulders. He's stands staring at her, motionless and in shock, not quite believing how different she looks.

Uncertainly, he says, 'Oh, um, Clarissa? Hello, I didn't see you there.'

'Hello Malcolm, my dear,' she replies cheerily. 'It's so nice to see you. Welcome to The Manse.'

Even the way she speaks strikes Malcolm as a little odd. Her voice sounds deeper than usual. His stomach lurches.

'Er, thanks,' he stutters. 'I um... like your house, it seems quite... big.'

'You are kind, Malcolm, thank you,' she purrs as she stands aside and makes a grand gesture of throwing her stick-like arm wide in welcome, opening the door fully so he can enter.

With a tight smile, he proceeds up the path and crosses the threshold into the house. As he enters, he turns to look at her and his smile falters as he sees her up close. Her eyes are solid black in the shadowy light. He frowns. *That's strange.* He could have sworn Clarissa had blue eyes, albeit with cataracts.

Entering the hall, the first thing that hits him is how cold it is. It feels like he's just stepped into an ice bath and he starts shivering. Looking around the large hall, he sees a grandfather clock, and what appeared at first to be table lamps are in fact candles in elaborate silver candlesticks. The floor is covered in large black and white tiles. *Ugh, awful.* It reminds him of a Victorian sanatorium he thinks as he eyeballs the many doors that lead off the hallway.

'This way my dear,' Clarissa says. 'I'm sure you'd like to see your room and get settled in before I show you around the house.' Clarissa gestures to the dark ornate staircase which runs up through the middle of the hall to the floor above.

Malcom manages a weak smile as he follows her up the stairs.

'Um, thanks, that would be nice,' he says. 'I, er, don't have a lot of stuff, really. Only here for a week and all that. So, I only brought what I thought I'd need.'

Malcolm trails off, aware that he's starting to mumble. His mum's words replay in his mind: 'Malcolm love,' she'd say, 'Don't mumble so, no one understands a word you're saying. No need to be shy!' Then she'd smile at him indulgently. He thinks about her smile now, and suddenly wishes he were at home with her, watching *Coronation Street* and listening to her rattle on about how bad the acting is these days.

As Clarissa leads Malcolm up the stairs, the surroundings make him feel unnerved. The house feels too quiet — in fact, it's deathly silent, and he doesn't like that it's so dark. Nothing like at Evergreen, which is full of light and drama, no matter what the hour is. There are candles everywhere. He's never seen the likes of it before. He wonders why she doesn't put the real lights on, but then he thinks maybe she isn't that well off after all. It's possible she's economising, just like he and his Mum have to.

Clarissa reaches the landing and looks back at him over her shoulder, signalling to a room on her left which has an ornate wooden door, with carvings of some sort all around the frame, he can't make them out clearly in the dim light. His unease is starting to build. There's a strange kind of aura about her. His stomach flips and he feels the urge to turn and flee. But instead, he just stands there, staring at her like an idiot, feeling awkward, alone and homesick in this strange, cold house.

Malcolm casts his eyes around the rest of the landing before entering his room. It mirrors the hall downstairs with numerous dark panelled doors on either side and candles mounted on the walls in between each door. Opposite the staircase is a floor-to-ceiling stained glass window. In the weak light, Malcolm can't make out the design, but he knows instinctively, even in daylight, he won't like it.

'Here you are, Malcolm,' Clarissa says. 'I hope you find the room comfortable. I'm sure you will. Many guests have stayed in this room over the years, and we've had such a lovely time with them.' She turns and smiles at him. Malcolm notes it doesn't quite reach her eyes. 'Please make yourself at home. I'll be back to show you the rest of the house once you've unpacked.'

With his hand on the doorknob, Malcolm turns to thank her and gasps. She's vanished. Astonished he looks around the hallway and back towards the staircase, but there's no sign of her. Nothing. Maybe she's gone into one of the rooms. *Of course*, he thinks. *Yes, that must be it.*

*One of the rooms must surely be her bedroom —
probably the one right opposite. Crikey though!
She's quick on her feet for her age.* He lets out a
sigh of relief and enters the room that will be his
home for the next week.

Dismay hits Malcom like a slap in the face.
'Oh my God — there's no TV!'

Scanning the rest of the room, he sees a
huge bed on the left, flanked either side by
bedside tables. A desk of some sort sits under
another stained-glass window, draped in heavy
curtains. The numerous candles lining the walls
would normally make a room look cosy, but it
reminds him of the inside of a crypt. With a
heavy heart, Malcolm sets his bag down on the
bed and starts to unpack the few things he
managed to grab in haste before setting off. He
realises with annoyance that he forgot to pack
his phone charger, but it should be okay for a
couple of days. Though he'll need to pop out at
some point to get another one if he wants to
speak to his mum during the week.

When he'd gone home earlier to pack, his
mum had already left for a hospital appointment
with her carer, Natalie. He'd left a note on the
kitchen table about his plans, but he would have
preferred to speak to her. He knows she worries
about him all the time.

Scrutinising the rest of the room, he sees
there's a solitary lightbulb hanging from the
ceiling. He finds the light switch by the door and

goes over to turn it on. Nothing. He flicks it again. Up. Down. Up. Down. Still nothing. *The bulb has probably blown*. He sighs. He'll have to remember to check it with Clarissa later.

Silently berating himself for being so impulsive and not checking everything about the job before he left, he starts to put his things away. He's just tucking his pyjamas inside the pillowcase like he does at home, when he feels a cold breath on the back of his neck, making his hair stand up on end.

Jumping, he turns around quickly. Clarissa is standing over by the door, nowhere near him.

'Oh!' Malcolm squeaks in shock. 'You made me jump. I didn't hear you come in.'

'So sorry, Malcolm my dear, I didn't mean to startle you. I did knock but you mustn't have heard me. You seemed to be miles away. I've come to show you your bathroom and the rest of the house.'

There was something in the way she spoke to him that made him feel like she was laughing at him.

*

Malcolm is standing in a cold, spacious bathroom. It's next door to his bedroom. The floor tiles match the ones in the hallway downstairs and there's a clawfoot free-standing bath in the middle of the room. No shower. Above the sink is a mottled mirror, and to the side, a decrepit stained toilet with a rusty pull-chain flush. A grimy window is set high into the wall opposite the door.

'So, now you've seen your rooms, we'll head downstairs and I'll show you the rest of the house,' says Clarissa, 'Then you can have a nice cup of tea and we can chat about everything else you'll need to know. Oh, and Malcolm dear, we do like our guests — so sorry, I mean our staff — to make use of the bathroom… every day,' she adds. She looks up at Malcolm and gives him an innocent-looking smile before making her way downstairs.

What a bloody cheek! He's never understood the need to shower every day, what's the bloody point? You only get dirty again, may as well leave it as long as possible, he's always thought. As he makes to follow her, he notices she's using a walking stick, clutching it as if her life depends on it, yet she seems steady enough on her legs. Still fuming after her comment, he stomps down the stairs after her.

Clarissa stops by a set of double doors behind the staircase. 'Here's the dining room. It's a beautiful room, and some of the furniture is, well, let's just say it's very old.'

No surprise there, Malcolm thinks wearily. *Everything in this bloody house is old.*

'Would you be so kind, Malcolm?' she says, her eyes indicating her walking stick.

'Oh, yeah, sorry, o' course.' Malcolm grabs both door handles. Not sure whether they open in or out, he gives them a firm push. They open inwards easily, and he nearly falls into the room.

'Oops, sorry,' he mutters, 'I, um thought they may be a little stiff.'

The dining room is typical of the rest of the rooms in The Manse. Large, cold and dimly lit. Candles adorn the walls, and the biggest dining table Malcolm has ever seen holds centre stage. *It's like something out of Downton Abbey,* he thinks as he looks around at the huge paintings of old castles and elaborate but somewhat macabre ornamental statues.

He notices the table is set for two.

'So, Malcolm, what do you think of it?'

'It's very big and um... very nice,' Malcolm responds. 'Did you like to um... entertain a lot then?'

Clarissa turns to Malcolm, a nostalgic look on her face. 'Oh yes! We used to have great feasts in this room. Sadly, there's hardly any of us left now. Only me and Herb–' Clarissa stops talking abruptly. 'Well, just me and a few others. Come along now, let's have that chat about what I'd like you to do whilst you're here.'

Chapter 9
Expectations

Malcolm is sat in what Clarissa calls the drawing room, drinking tea. A quaint tea-set is laid out in front of him on a small ornate coffee table. He struggles to keep hold of the tiny cup handle as his thumb and forefinger are too big to hold it securely. He notices Clarissa is not joining him. He recalls now that when she was at the care home, she'd barely eaten or drunk anything, and when she did, she nearly always got a funny tummy. She dismissed it afterwards as having a delicate digestive system, and the number of times he'd witnessed her being sick was testament to that.

Clarissa has just shown Malcolm the kitchen, which was a bit of a shock. It was cold, like the rest of the house, but there were no signs of cooking, food items or indeed daily use which had surprised him. It was certainly dated; there was a long oblong slab of butcher's wood that served as an island in the middle of the room, an ugly old-fashioned Aga stood opposite the sink, and although kitchen cupboards were where you'd expect them to be, they appeared mainly empty.

There was a huge chest freezer next to the back door, which she'd asked Malcolm to open and count how many pieces of clingfilm-wrapped food parcels were left inside, explaining that they were her daily frozen food meals. Malcolm would need to take out two portions each morning to thaw, then serve them for her evening meal. Malcolm had peered down into the freezer and counted four pieces of what he suspected was frozen chicken. Other than that, there was nothing else in there, and he couldn't understand why she needed such a large freezer. Maybe she was just getting low on food. She might well ask him to go shopping, he thought hopefully. That would give him a chance to get a new phone charger.

She'd gone on to show him where the rudimentary items such as tea, coffee and sugar were. A fridge had a limited selection of foodstuffs, such as milk and cheese. Another cupboard contained tins and crackers, but other than that there wasn't much in the way of food. *Jesus!* He was going to starve at this rate.

Malcolm had kept tight-lipped, though. He understood only too well about having to economise. He was very careful with the small amount of money he and his mum had to live on. He bought all their food from budget supermarkets. The only luxury food they allowed themselves was a couple of cream cakes on a Saturday night while they watched their favourite TV programmes.

'So, now you've seen everything, Malcolm. Have you any questions, my dear?'

Clarissa sits opposite him in an enormous, wingback chair, which he thinks makes her look ridiculous, whilst Malcolm perches on the end of an ancient, overstuffed armchair. Clarissa clutches her walking stick as Malcolm clutches his cup of tea.

Clarissa looks at him expectantly. 'Malcolm?'

He had been thinking how demented she looked, sitting there gripping her walking stick possessively, as if it were her purse that contained her bingo winnings.

Malcolm looks blankly back at her. 'Sorry, what did you say?'

'I said,' Clarissa says slowly, a slight irritated tone creeping into her voice, 'Do you have any questions?'

'Oh, um... no. Well, actually yeah, I just wondered if you could fix the light in my bedroom. It's not working, see? And, well,' Malcolm rushes on before he loses the courage to ask her anything else. 'I know you said you want me to thaw your chicken every night, but what shall I serve with it? Cos I only saw a few things in the cupboard and they, um, won't last a week and, um... I just wondered if that meant you wanted me to go out and do some shopping for you. Which I don't mind at all… cos you see I could do with popping to the shops myself…'

The lack of a TV flashes into his head, but Malcolm trails off, acutely aware that his nervousness is making him talk too quickly and he hasn't given her a chance to answer.

Clarissa looks straight at him, then suddenly throws her head back and laughs hysterically.

It's an awful, guttural sound.

Malcolm jumps at her reaction. Thinking he must have said something funny, he starts to laugh too, but it's a nervous laugh, and soon putters out as he realises how deranged Clarissa looks and sounds. He grips his now stone-cold cup of tea trying to stop his hand from shaking slightly.

Suddenly, Clarissa stops laughing, as abruptly as she'd started, and stares at him.

'Now, don't worry about anything, dear,' Clarissa says. 'Everything will be fine. The light switch in your bedroom must be playing up again, I'll get it fixed. In fact, I remember the last…' She suddenly stops talking, then continues, 'As for the food, you are sweet to be so considerate, but really there's no need to worry. In a couple of nights — I mean, tomorrow — the freezer will be full again and our… stocks… I mean, our food delivery will arrive. So, as I say, no need to concern yourself with that.'

'Oh, so, when it arrives... What else would you like to eat apart from chicken? I mean, would you like me to do some veggies to go with your evening meal? And what time do you want me to bring you your tea and biscuits?'

As he waits for her to respond, it dawns on him that he too would be limited in the food department until the delivery. *Was he expected to only eat chicken too? God almighty, he knows he needs to lose weight, but after a week of this, there'll be nothing left of him. He'd just have to eat what was in the cupboard for now.*

'Chicken?' Clarissa asks, looking somewhat puzzled. 'What on earth...?' Then, 'Oh!' she exclaims, as something seems to dawn on her. 'Ah yes, of course, the chicken in the freezer, yes, yes, I see.' Clarissa stifles a laugh. 'Well, you know me, Malcolm. We, I mean, *I* don't tend to drink or eat much of anything. As you know, I have a very delicate constitution and there are only certain foods I can eat, so there'll be no need for any extras. Meat is just fine.'

'Yeah, I did notice you didn't eat much when you were at Evergreen,' Malcolm says, 'but I thought that was just Chef's cooking. Okay, well if you're sure then.' He's amazed at how little food she survives on, thinking of his mum, who has a hearty appetite, despite her age — well, certainly when it comes to cream cakes.

'Also, whilst we're on the subject of food', Clarissa continues. 'You will have noticed in the dining room that the table was set for two.'

Malcolm realises she is waiting for him to say something, so nods and says, 'Oh yeah, o' course, very fancy dinner plates they were too. Are they silver? And where do you want me to put them after we've finished eating our dinner? In that fancy cabinet in the dining room?'

'*Our* dinner?' Clarissa almost shrieks.

'Um…'

His cheeks flare crimson with embarrassment. 'Well, I thought with two places set, and me being your companion and all that, we would have to… erm… I mean that you'd want me to eat with you in the evenings and keep you company. But I don't have to eat your food. O' course I'm happy to eat my own, I'll just need to do a bit of shopping and…'

'I'm sorry, Malcolm, I should have explained earlier,' she says with a bemused smile. 'I don't expect you to eat with me in the evenings. You can eat your meals in the kitchen. In fact, I was just about to tell you that I don't live here alone. My husband Herbert lives here too, but he spends most of his time in bed as he's much older than me and can't always get up. But when he can, he occasionally joins me for dinner. All I ask of you is that you ensure that the er… chicken has been defrosted from the freezer in the morning and that it's plated up and left in the dining room for eleven-thirty tonight.'

'Eleven-thirty!' exclaims Malcolm. Then, feeling embarrassed for cutting her off mid-sentence, says, 'Um, sorry, it's just that's, um, that's quite late, are you sure—'

'We've always eaten late in the evening,' Clarissa interrupts abruptly. 'It... helps us to sleep.

'Oh, sorry, I just thought...' He's lost for words and feels quite stupid and doesn't quite understand why she needs a companion. If all that's required of him is to defrost a bit of bloody chicken. There must be something he's missing. He feels sure there's something she hasn't told him. Probably a whole load of other stuff he'd rather not do. 'Is there anything else?'

Malcolm looks at her expectantly.

'Well,' she says brightly, 'I'm glad you mention that, because yes, there are some odd jobs around the house and some cleaning I'd like you to do. For a start I need you to clean the entire kitchen, it needs a good scrub from top to bottom, and most importantly all the cutlery, especially the knives, they're a little... dirty, so I'd like you to make sure they're nice and shiny. Oh, and you'll notice that the front and back doors are always kept locked, and they must remain so. It's to keep Herbert... safe. He can sometimes... well he sometimes wakes and gets confused and I don't want him wandering outside. I won't need a lot of company as my dear Herbert is not too well at the moment, so I'll need to keep a close eye on him, so I suggest you use the study when you're not needed. I haven't shown it you yet — there's a small TV in there you can watch, but it's where we keep some of our most treasured and valuable books, Malcolm, so if you do want to use the room then please, I must insist that you do not touch any of the books.'

'Oh, thank God! Erm, I mean, thank you!' Malcolm exclaims. He feels so relieved knowing that there's a TV in the house that he lets out a sigh and gives her a big smile. *Maybe things aren't going to be so dire after all and besides, it's only for a week.*

Chapter 10
Next of Kin

Archie has been rushed off his feet all day and is clearing up some paperwork on his desk. He's hoping to leave on time for once — it's Friday night after all, and he'd promised his wife Angie that he'd be home in time for dinner.

As he slaps his laptop closed, a yellow sticky note wafts off his desk onto the floor. Picking it up, he realises it's the one about Malcolm. He sighs. 'Shit, I nearly forgot,' he murmurs under his breath.

Pulling his mobile phone out of his jacket pocket, he dials the number. As he waits for someone to answer, he steps over to the filing cabinet that holds the staff files and yanks the top drawer open. With the phone cradled between his ear and his shoulder, he flips through the folders until he finds the file titled *Banner, Malcolm*.

'Hello?' a small tremulous voice says suddenly in his ear. 'Is that you, Malcolm love?'

'Oh, hello, no, it's Archie Barrington. I'm calling from Evergreen Care Home. You left a message about Malcolm?' Archie says as he returns to his seat and opens Malcolm's file.

'Hello, Malcolm? Is that you?' the voice asks again, more tentatively now.

Archie is in no mood for this after the day he's had. He feels a tension headache coming on.

'No, this is *not* Malcolm. My name is Archie Barrington, I'm Malcolm's boss,' he says impatiently. 'Can you tell me who you are and how I can help you?' As he waits for her response, he finds the page where Malcolm's next of kin details should be listed, and to his annoyance he sees the page is blank.

'Oh, hello Marty!' the voice on the other end of the line says. 'I was looking for Malcolm. Sorry — I'm a bit deaf, dear. Oh dear, maybe I should put my hearing aid in,' she says to herself. Then, 'Shall I put my hearing aid in?'

God Almighty! Archie fumes. He doesn't need this now. It's all he can do not to snap. Keeping his voice in check, he speaks slowly, 'It's A r c h i e,' annunciating each letter of his name as clearly as he can, '*not* M a r t y.' Then realises it probably doesn't matter; she can't hear him anyway. Exasperated, he continues, 'You called this number looking for Malcolm and I was wondering who you were and what you needed him for?' he says, trying to sound somewhat gentler.

'Oh, silly me! Yes, hello Marty, you must be his boss then. Well, can you tell him his Mum needs to talk to him urgently? I need to tell him what the doctor at the hospital said to me today. You see, I'm under that doctor with the funny name and, well, you see he wanted to know some things — the doctor that is — but I weren't sure what to tell him. Only my Malcolm would know what to say, see?'

Archie cuts in quickly, 'Did you say you're Malcolm's mum?

'Hello? Hello, are you there, Marty? I can't hear you very well dear, I'm a bit deaf you see.'

'Yes, yes. I can hear you and I'm still here!' he snaps, his patience momentarily getting the better of him again.

'He told me he had to go and do a posh job for a lady in London,' she continues, completely ignoring his question. 'Somewhere on the tube. But see, the doctor — you know, the one with the funny name at the hospital — says he needs to talk to him urgently on Monday. I've been trying to call him, but he's not answering. Can you tell him for me, Marty? Hello? Marty, are you there?'

This is going nowhere fast. Archie lets out a groan.

'Of course I can, Mrs Banner. I'll call him on his mobile phone,' he says more gently. 'The thing is, it's quite late now and I'm about to leave the office...'

'What's that, Marty? *You* have his mobile phone? Why on earth would he give you his mobile phone? Oh dear,' she says, her voice rising in panic. 'He knows he needs his phone so he can call me, see? He always calls me to check — oh dear…'

'No, no — *I* don't have his mobile phone, Mrs Banner,' Archie says, frustrated. *Lord give me patience.* She's starting to sound tearful. He has to get a hold of this conversation quickly if he wants to get out of here before midnight.

With all the patience he can muster, he says, 'It's okay, Mrs Banner, I *don't* have his phone but I promise I will get him to call you as soon as possible. No need to worry, I'm sure he'll call you soon.'

Archie knows that he probably won't get the chance to call Malcolm before Monday, given the plans he's got for the weekend with his family, but his mum doesn't need to know that. 'Is that okay, Mrs Banner?'

'I see. I'm sorry dear, I'm a bit deaf you see. So, you'll tell my Malcolm will you Marty? So that he knows he needs to talk to the doctor with the funny name on Monday, is that what you're saying?'

'Yes, yes, I'll do that Mrs Banner, now don't you worry, I'm sure he'll be in touch soon.'

'Thank you, Marty, it was nice speaking to you'

Archie gets up and puts Malcolm's file back in the drawer. It's the first weekend in months that he's not on call and he really doesn't want to have to deal with any work issues if he can help it. He'd promised his wife and daughter that he wouldn't take any work issues home with him this weekend. But then again, Malcolm being at Clarissa's is hardly a normal work issue, given his involvement and the unscrupulous way in which he'd arranged it, he'd get sacked if head office found out about the deal he'd made. Sighing, he realises he'll have to call him later tonight.

Grabbing his car keys, he leaves the office.

Chapter 11
Incubus – Succubus

He doesn't know how Clarissa fixed the light without coming into his room, but thankfully it is now working. Malcolm lies on the huge bed, chewing his nails, contemplating the conversation with Clarissa in the drawing room. He frowns, still feeling perplexed. He doesn't know what a real companion is meant to do — not outside of the care home, anyway — but he knows that what is being asked of him here isn't quite right. He's decided he doesn't like Clarissa and he certainly doesn't like this house, both of which give him the creeps, but for the money she's paying him, there is no way he can back out now. He needs the money desperately, otherwise how else is he going to fulfil the promise he made to his mum? *And anyway, it's only for a week*, he thinks, consoling himself.

As he looks upwards, he notices there are marks all over the ceiling. Frowning, he stands up to take a closer look. It looks like someone has used a dirty sweeping brush and swiped the ceiling with it. The marks are thin and seem to glisten, reminding him of shimmery silver slug trails. 'Ugh!' *That's the last bloody thing I need.* He shivers at the thought of a slug slithering up his body whilst he's asleep.

Shuffling around the room, he inspects the carpet and walls. Satisfied there are no slugs anywhere, he picks up his phone to check the time. *Typical! No bloody signal and only two per cent left on the battery.* He sighs. It's only seven-thirty pm. He puts the phone back on the bedside table. *Hmm, what shall I do now?* Plonking himself down on the bed, he checks the state of his badly bitten nails. He doesn't really want to go downstairs just yet, and wishes ruefully that he'd brought something to read. His tummy starts rumbling, and despite storming through all the crisps and chocolate bars he'd brought with him in the last half an hour, he still feels famished. Knowing he's got nothing to do until about eleven pm, when he'll need to set the food out in the dining room, he decides to go and see if he can find something to eat, then maybe watch a bit of TV in the study. As he makes his way downstairs, he thinks back to his conversation with Clarissa earlier. He hadn't realised her husband Herbert also lived in the house — how strange she hadn't mentioned him whilst she was at the care home. He wondered how on earth she managed to get him from the bedroom, which he presumed was upstairs, all the way down the stairs and into the dining room, given he was so old and fragile. Maybe tonight Clarissa would ask him to help.

*

Happier now, having found some cheese and crackers to eat, he thinks cheekily it would be nice to have something to wash it down with. He hums to himself as he starts to check the kitchen cupboards. 'Aha!' Reaching in, he takes out a dusty wine bottle. He can't tell if it's red or white because the label has completely faded and the bottle is almost black. He peeks over his shoulder at the kitchen door. *May as well try it. No harm in that, surely?* He thinks cheekily. He scrabbles about in the drawers and finds a rusty corkscrew, then takes down a goblet-style wine glass from another cupboard. The cork is well and truly stuck. It takes all his strength to get it to budge, but after much pulling and tugging, and placing the bottle between his thighs, he eventually hears a satisfying pop! *Finally!* He pulls the corkscrew out and starts to pour wine into the glass, but annoyingly nothing comes out. He tuts, tipping the wine bottle upside down and shaking it. Still, nothing comes out. Peering into the neck of the bottle, he realises a bit of cork has broken off and got stuck.

'Oh, for heaven's sake.'

Taking a knife from one of the drawers, he starts jabbing downwards to try and dislodge it. Suddenly, the knife goes right down and red wine spurts out, making a puddle on the counter and soaking the cuff of his jumper. He mops up the kitchen counter before scoffing the cheese and crackers and guzzling down the wine.

*

In the study, he swipes the crumbs from his mouth as he looks around the room. There's a comfy looking armchair and a small TV perched on an antique chest opposite. It's a smallish room; the walls are covered with floor-to-ceiling bookshelves that make Malcolm feel more than a little claustrophobic. Apart from his local library, he's never seen so many books in one room, some of which are so large and heavy the middle of the bookshelves are bending perilously from the sheer weight of them. He feels sure if he so much as touches one, the whole lot will collapse. Going as close as he dares, he takes a closer look at the titles, noticing that hardly any of them are in English. One book catches his eye — it has large fancy gold lettering on its spine. Holding his breath, he takes a cautious step nearer to get a closer look. The last thing he wants is to have the whole lot come tumbling down on top of him.

'*Incubus — Succubus Through the Middle Ages* by H. Meyer.' He repeats the title phonetically, 'In - cu – bus - suck - u - bus.' He giggles. 'What the hell is… In – cu - bus and Succ - u - bus?' Shaking his head, he continues to roll the word around his mouth, 'Suck u bus, suck u bus, suc u—'

'Malcolm!'

Malcolm jerks around, almost cricking his neck as he twirls towards the voice. Clarissa is standing in the doorway, staring at him. A look of pure rage on her face.

Dropping her head sideways so that it lies parallel to her shoulder at a right angle, she whispers menacingly, 'Malcolm, did I not make myself clear earlier? I told you not to go anywhere near those books. Why did you defy me?'

Malcolm gapes at her as he takes in the horrific image. The dim candlelight from the hallway silhouettes her skeletal facial features, her white hair is wild, reminding him of Medusa, and her black, venomous eyes are boring into him. *Oh God, she's completely mad, she's… she's…* His mind searches for the right word: *deranged.* Worse, he realises, as his body breaks out in a sweat, she looks like the bloody devil himself.

Shaking and humiliated, he continues to stare mutely at her. His mouth has gone bone dry and he can't seem to get his tongue to form any words. He looks at the floor as he twiddles his fingers and tries to stop the muscles in his legs from trembling. Fright at the sight of her and shame at being caught out send anxiety whooshing through his body like mini punches to his gut. *To hell with this, I want to go home. She can keep her money.*

As Malcolm stands transfixed, a rising sense of outrage replaces his fear. He stands a little straighter and raises his chin in defiance. Finding his voice at last, he says, 'Um... actually, well, to be honest, Clarissa... I... um, I don't think this is working out too well. For either of us. So... I think it's best I just leave. I won't spend a penny of your money, you have my word. I'm going to get my things now and I'll ask Archie to send you someone else for the rest of the week.' His heart hammers in his chest as Clarissa continues to glare at him. Her black pupils appear to be fading in and out, reminding him of a kaleidoscope he once found.

Feeling somewhat emboldened now he's spoken, he throws his shoulders back and stomps from the room, but the sudden momentum that drives him forward makes him clumsy, and as he lurches through to the hall, he accidentally leaves Clarissa half spinning in the doorway. Feeling appalled at his outburst but not caring anymore, he marches on towards the staircase.

'Malcolm! Malcolm! My dear,' Clarissa screeches as she teeters after him, her heels clattering on the tiled floor. She manages to catch up to him at the foot of the staircase.

'Malcolm! I'm sorry, my dear. I... I can only apologise. I'm not quite myself, you see, it's... it's Herbert, he's... he's not very well!' she blurts. 'Please forgive me. I'm so sorry, I don't know what came over me, I shouldn't have spoken to you like that, I see that now, but you see if anything happens to my Herbert, well... I don't know if I could go on living. Please don't leave us...' she says, suddenly sounding timid — childlike even.

Malcolm turns, one hand on the banister. Clarissa is looking up at him tearfully, but no tears fall. He realises now how vulnerable, weak, and frail she looks; more ridiculous than scary.

He lets out a deep sigh thinking of his mum and why he's here in the first place and his face softens.

'Um, well... Okay. I suppose we could see how we get on for now — but I promise you, I didn't touch your books. 'Let's just see—'

'Oh, thank you! Of course you didn't, dear! I know that now, I'm just being a silly old woman. There's no need to leave, no need at all,' she interjects quickly, smiling placatingly at him before he can say anything else. 'Why don't you go and watch a bit of TV while I go and change for dinner?' she says. 'You'd like that, wouldn't you?'

He thinks again about the money and how much he needs it for his mum. 'Um... well, okay — s'pose,' he says reluctantly. *After all*, he thinks, *what's he got to lose? But if she loses it again, he'll definitely leave.*

He turns from the staircase and starts trundling back towards the study, but once he hears Clarissa climbing the stairs, he decides to go straight to the kitchen to find some more morsels to nibble on.

As Malcolm sits watching the TV, having finished off the hard cheese, dodgy looking crackers and iffy red wine, he starts thinking: if — and it's a big if — he does decide to stay till the end of the week, he'll need to go and get some food shopping for himself tomorrow, especially now he's polished off most of what was in the kitchen.

Chapter 12
The Party

'Dad! Please can I go? Pleeease? Pretty please? Mum, tell him, if I don't go to Melanie's party, no one will speak to me again — like, ever!' Evie whines as she starts clearing the table.

Archie sighs. He's used to being treated like a taxi driver by his sixteen-year-old daughter, but he's not sure about this particular party. First of all, he doesn't like the fancy dress outfit she intends to wear, and secondly, he's sure there'll be alcohol available, despite what Evie says.

Archie glances over at his wife, Angie, who's suddenly become very interested in stacking the dishwasher, then looks up at his daughter — her expression silently pleading. 'Oh, okay,' he says resignedly, 'But I'm warning you, Evie — absolutely no alcohol. If I get so much as a whiff of it on you, you'll be grounded for a year, is that clear?'

Evie's response is to squeal in delight, almost puncturing Archie's eardrum.

'Yes, I promise I will. I mean, I won't! And thanks, Dad, you're the best!' she says as she grabs her phone off the table and bolts towards her bedroom.

'Hang on a sec,' Archie says, 'Where is it again?'

'It's in Canehill somewhere, not far from the high street. I'll send you Melanie's address in a sec so you can look it up,' Evie says without breaking her stride.

Archie looks over at Angie. She's shaking her head and trying not to smile.

'What?'

'She has you wrapped around her little finger,' Angie says as she comes over to the table and plants a kiss on his forehead.

'Canehill. I'm sure that's where Malcolm is... Which reminds me, I'm just going to make a quick call,' he says. Picking up his phone, he scrolls through his contacts as he makes his way to the living room and pulls up Malcolm's details.

'I'm sorry, the person you are calling cannot take your call right now. Please leave a message after the tone...' He hits redial and gets the same message. Hits redial again. This time, he says, 'Hi Malcolm, this is Archie from work. Could you, er... give me a call please when you get this message? Nothing to worry about, it's just I have a message from your um... Mum. I'll try again later, or, um, just call her — but also let me know that you've received this message. Okay? Thanks. Bye.'

Chapter 13
Just a Dream

His lips are sticky from the red wine. He uses the cuff of his jumper to clean them as he scans the bookshelves, his eyes settling on the book title he was looking at when Clarissa came in and scolded him like a schoolboy. Still quietly fuming at the way she'd spoken to him; he creeps over to the bookshelf. He doesn't know what the hell an incubus or succubus is, and decides he'll look it up when he next visits the library. He can't see anything else here he thinks would interest him. Deflated, he turns to put the TV on, but as he does, he catches sight of a small black door clasp at the end of the middle bookshelf. Peering at it closely, he sees it belongs to a small door. If you didn't know it was already there, you'd never notice it. *Maybe it's a secret room like they had years ago for hiding priests.* He looks for the keyhole but there isn't one. He pushes hard against it. Nothing gives — it's solid, like it's been bricked up on the other side. He lets out a nonchalant grunt and sits down to relax in front of the TV. He can feel the effects of the red wine making him drowsy, and as he allows the mundane travel programme to wash over him. He's only half aware that he's nodding off to sleep, as he tries but fails to stay awake.

He's suddenly aware of a strange sensation in his lower body. It stirs a long-lost memory of pleasure and brings a small smile to his lips. The stirrings continue to rouse him, and as he wakes fully and opens his eyes, he yells out in shock.

Clarissa is straddled on top of him, gyrating around his crotch and laughing manically. Her obscene red lips are open, revealing razor-sharp teeth, and her black, demonic eyes seem to paralyse him as she continues to writhe over his private parts. Screaming, he leaps up, which makes his head spin. He feels so sick and dizzy that he nearly keels over. Disgusted and ashamed of himself, he realises he was just dreaming —probably a result of drinking the revolting red wine he'd found in the kitchen cupboard. As his ardour deflates, he shakes his head, trying to rid himself of the mental image now seared into his mind. Checking his phone, he sees it's much later than he thought. He'll have to hurry if he wants to get the food ready on time.

*

Malcolm gazes around the dining room, checking everything is in order, and feels a small sense of pride. He wishes his mum could see the place. Yeah, sure, it's a bit creepy and old, but it is without a doubt the grandest place he's ever been in. He's set the foul-smelling food out on the fancy dinner plates, he gave it a sniff earlier and it neither looks nor smells like any chicken he's ever tasted. Still, the soft candlelight is making the plates sparkle and it reminds him of some fancy dish that you might get in a very fancy restaurant. Realising he's forgotten the cutlery, he goes to the dresser, and as he's laying them out he notices there's a large iron ring fixed to the edge of the table. He circles the table slowly; there are five rings in total — one at the top, two at the bottom, and one on either side.

What the...? His stomach flips as he thinks about what the rings may have been used for in the past. Closing the doors, he exits the room as quick as he can, clambering clumsily up the stairs to his bedroom.

*

Lying in bed, Malcolm can hear the wind howling like a banshee outside the bedroom window. The rain smacks against the windowpane insistently, as if it's knocking to get in. There's a storm on the way, he recalls now the weather report this week, which predicted a severe storm coming down from the north, just in time for the weekend.

Malcolm's eyes are wide open and fixed on the bedroom door. The curtains are fully open, the ceiling light is on, and the candles are all alight, despite his fear of them falling onto the carpet and setting the room on fire. *I'd rather burn to death than let that woman come anywhere near me.*

His mind is racing as he thinks over everything that's happened since his arrival. Clarissa's strange way of talking. The way she looks so different here. *And a husband? Where the hell in the house is he? Maybe she's keeping him prisoner? Oh God, maybe he's dead but she's got him stuffed in an armchair in one of the bedrooms. Shit — he could even be in the room opposite. And what about that old dining table, with the iron rings all around it? What the hell is that all about? It feels so sinister.* 'Get a grip!' Malcolm says, mentally admonishing himself for letting his mind run away with itself. He continues to stare at the bedroom door, and to try and settle his mind, he starts picturing his mum's reaction when he gives her the good news at the end of the week. He can't wait to see her face light up.

He must have fallen asleep because something jolts him awake. Staring at the door, he realises something isn't right. He feels the hair on the back of his neck stand up and his skin starts prickling all over his body. His breathing becomes heavy, and his heart starts beating wildly. The ceiling light is no longer on; the dim candlelight is casting eerie shadows around the room. He can't move, and fear pushes down on him, threatening to crush all the air from his lungs.

Just then, something wet plops on to his shoulder. Swivelling his eyes, he sees a glistening blob of saliva still attached to what looks like some sort of glutinous thread, dangling from above. He squints up into the darkness. As his brain catches up with what he sees above him, his eyes nearly pop from their sockets. A scream freezes in his throat as terror paralyses him. There's a long body on the ceiling. Its head is twisted backwards, facing the wrong way, and staring straight at him. It has unnaturally elongated limbs and its claw like feet and hands appear to be suckered to the ceiling. Thick saliva is dripping from the black hole that is its mouth. Tissue-thin skin stretches across a skeletal white face, accentuating ghastly protruding cheekbones, its hate filled silver pupils emphasise the black void that lays beyond, as it stares down at him.

The creature slowly opens its mouth wider and Malcolm can see candlelight reflecting off its black pointed teeth. Then it lets out an ear-piercing scream.

Malcolm jerks upwards, as though his body has just received a massive electric shock, and a raspy roar dies in his throat as he's brutally torn from his nightmare. He stumbles out of bed, dazed and terrified. Frantically scanning the ceiling and the rest of the room for the demonic creature, it's only then he feels the warm, wet liquid seeping down his legs.

Chapter 14
Herbert

'Darling. You're a silly man! What were you thinking? Come down from there at once and get back into bed.'

Herbert keens miserably in response. Looking down on Clarissa from the ceiling, he flicks his forked tongue impatiently around his mouth, which is dripping with saliva.

'I know you're hungry, but you haven't got long to wait now my love. You know the rules. You can't eat until the thirteenth hour. It's a very special night for us, you mustn't spoil it again. Now, come and lay beside me and try to settle down,' Clarissa says, trying to soothe him.

Herbert jumps from the ceiling onto the floor and slides his lithe body into bed beside Clarissa as she starts to hum an old Hungarian love song.

'I'm hungry,' Herbert growls. 'I must eat.'

'I know darling, soon.'

'I'm hungry, I must eat.'

Clarissa resumes humming.

'There, there,' she whispers.

Chapter 15
The Morning After

Malcolm wakes stiff and groggy, snippets of the horrific nightmare still fresh in his mind. Plodding over to the window, he checks the weather. Dark storm clouds envelop the house and all the way to the horizon. It's still raining — heavily. He checks the time on his phone; it's early. He clocks the amount of battery left, *shit, only one per cent and still no signal.* He'll have to get to the shops on the high street today so he can get another charger and call his mum.

He spies his damp, crumpled pyjama bottoms lying in a heap on the floor and a wave of shame hits him as he remembers how terrified he was. It felt so real, so vivid. He can still see the creature's piercing silver eyes glaring at him with malice, its black pointed teeth ready to tear into his face. His body lets out an involuntary shiver, as if someone has walked over his grave. *It must be this house, it's so bloody creepy. Clarissa is just as creepy and God only knows what that husband of hers is like. He's still a mystery. Maybe I'll find out today.* He picks up his pyjama bottoms. He'll need to rinse them out in the bathroom and hopefully they will have dried by bedtime.

*

Malcolm has taken the last two pieces of meat out of the chest freezer in the kitchen and laid them out to thaw. As he clears the table from last night's dinner, he notices how clean the plates and glasses are. Spotless, you might say, but he washes them anyway and puts them back in the dresser, all the while eyeing up the iron rings around the table. Just looking at them gives him the heebie jeebies, but after a few moments, curiosity gets the better of him and he can't resist touching the one nearest to him. He's shocked at how heavy it feels. *God Almighty! What on earth are they doing on a dining table?* Feeling quite sickened, he drops it quickly and winces as it thuds loudly against the table.

 'Malcolm?'

 He nearly jumps out of his skin.

 Clarissa is standing in the open doorway.

 God! I wish she wouldn't keep creeping up on me like that.

 'Er, hello Clarissa, I didn't realise you were up and about.'

 'Yes, well occasionally I get up early if Herbert is sleeping soundly, and last night, well, he didn't sleep that well. In fact, he had quite a disturbed night. But it won't last, he just gets a little agitated when we have visitors in the house. He'll get used to it. He's sleeping now,' Clarissa says, smiling at him mysteriously.

'I thought we could have a cup of tea in the drawing room,' she continues as she turns and walks into the hallway.

Malcolm notices that this morning she's wearing a long, dark purple dress which has bizarre silver symbols on it. Her white, straw like hair looks wild, reminding him of an ageing rock star that should have given up years ago. She's using her walking stick too, but like yesterday, she seems as nimble as a gazelle.

'Yup, just coming,' he says, hoping this will give him the chance to tell her that he needs to go out.

'So, how was your first night, Malcolm? I hope you slept well?' Clarissa is sat in her wingback chair again, looking as ridiculous as ever.

'Um, well actually... I didn't sleep that well. I had a—'

Clarissa looks intently at Malcolm and appears to hold her breath.

Oh no, he thinks, *did she hear me shout out last night?*

Malcolm continues, 'Probably cos, you know, um, it was my first night here. I'm sure I'll have a better night's sleep tonight.'

'Well of course you will!' Clarissa replies. 'It's not easy settling into a new house and a new job. It's bound to feel a bit strange. But I hope nothing disturbed you?' Clarissa peers closely at him.

Malcolm squirms under her intense scrutiny, her eyes boring into him as she waits for his answer. The demonic creature from Malcolm's nightmare once again flashes through his mind's eye.

He swallows. 'Um, no, nothing disturbed me, just a bad dream is all,' Malcolm says, hoping the fear he felt last night is not showing on his face.

'Oh good, I'm pleased,' Clarissa replies.

'Um, before I forget,' Malcolm rushes on, 'I'll need to pop out to the high street today. I forgot to pack something important and, well, I just wondered if you would like me to get you anything whilst I'm out?'

'*Oh*... Wh... what on earth do you need to get that is so important?' Clarissa asks, a little sharply.

'Well... um, I really should have brought some food with me, and, well, I forgot to bring my phone charger and, um...' Malcolm retrieves his teacup from the coffee table. 'So, if you want, I can pick up—'

'Food? Clarissa asks, sounding surprised, then pauses in thought before continuing. 'Yes, I suppose a big man... I mean a healthy man like yourself must have quite an appetite! I see. Yes, of course. I must admit that was an oversight on my part, Malcolm. I'm sorry, what must you think of me?'

'It's no bother,' Malcolm says. 'I'm happy to pick up anything you might need—'

"Well, the thing is, it's our anniversary tonight, and as I say, I'm expecting a delivery myself, and you will *need* to be here for that as I won't be able to manage it on my own. I'm just not sure what time it will arrive…' Clarissa says, as she appears to consider the situation.

Malcolm's tea is stone cold now, so he puts the cup back down on the coffee table.

Clarissa continues, 'Maybe after the delivery you could go to the shops? Would that suit you?'

'Yeah, well, I suppose that would be okay, as long as the delivery comes before the shops close. See, I really do need to get a charger, or I won't be able to call my—'

'Of course, I understand, Malcolm,' Clarissa cuts in. 'Right then, that's settled, you can go *after* the delivery. In the meantime, maybe you'd be good enough to clean the kitchen and all the cutlery in the kitchen drawer today? And maybe a bit of a spring clean in the dining room? Herbert will be… I mean, I'm hoping Herbert will feel well enough to join me for dinner tonight. It's a special night for us,' Clarissa says, beaming at Malcom. It's the first time he's ever seen her really smile. Ordinarily that would be nice, except it makes her look even creepier.

'Oh, and Malcolm,' she adds, 'Please do eat anything you like from the fridge and whatever else you find in the cupboards. That should tide you over until you can get out to the shops, shouldn't it?'

'Um, yeah, I guess… Thanks, I'm sure I'll be okay until then.' *That's if I'm not already dead from starvation*, he thinks ruefully.

Chapter 16
Anniversary

So, it's their anniversary. No wonder Clarissa seems more jaunty than usual. It's nice to think that two people, no matter how old they get, can still feel happy about their wedding anniversary. He should have asked her how long they'd been married. Maybe he'll ask her later, and who knows — maybe he'll even get to see Herbert tonight.

For some reason, the thought of Clarissa's wedding anniversary makes him think of his mum. She never had the chance to get married. As far as he knew, his dad had run out on her the minute she'd told him she was pregnant with Malcolm. Sometimes, when he's feeling down, the thought of what his dad did really hurts. It feels like his heart is being crushed. But then he reasons: if he's never known the love of a father, how can not having one hurt him? He suspects it's more to do with the hurt he feels on behalf of his mum. She's been a loving mum to him all his life and he doesn't need anyone else — that's why he can't wait to get home at the end of the week and tell her they'll be off to Ireland.

Galway, Ireland. That's all she's talked about — for years now. That and the younger brother she'd left behind, Patrick. She seems to reminisce even more now that her health is failing. Patrick still lives in the same house they were born and grew up in. He'd never married or had a family, but they'd kept in touch over the years. He had crippling arthritis, so couldn't travel far and with his mum's multiple sclerosis, they hadn't seen each other since she'd left home. She'd been saying for years that she could die happy if she could just see her little brother's face again, and although Malcolm couldn't bear the thought of losing her, he wants more than anything to grant her that wish.

That's why this job and the money he'll get paid for it means so much to him. Ireland isn't the other side of the world, but they've never had a lot in life and only just managed to scrape by each week. There's never enough money left over to save for anything, but this job has given him the opportunity to pay for their flights and at least a small amount of spending money. He can't wait to see her reaction when he tells her she can finally visit her little brother.

Malcolm checks his phone, the signal has one bar and the battery is still showing one per cent. He'll have to hold off calling his mum until he's got a new charger and charged it for a while and he'll probably have to go outside to get a signal. Hopefully Clarissa's delivery will turn up soon, then he can get out. He's already eaten most of the food in the cupboards and there are only a few things left. Just then, he notices the voice message icon flashing. He doesn't recognise the number but hits the 'play message' button anyway and hopes it won't totally kill the battery.

He's surprised to hear Archie's voice, and even more surprised to hear that his mum has called his work number and left a message with him.

'Shit', he mutters, trying to think what to do for the best. Firstly, he realises that Archie now knows that Malcolm didn't mention that he's a secondary carer on his job application form. There was an entire page on the form about personal details and next of kin that he should have completed. The form asked questions about caring responsibilities but Malcolm had deliberately left it blank as he thought it would ruin his chances of getting the job. He now wonders anxiously if that means he's going to get the sack.

He plonks himself down on the bed, running a hand through his greasy hair as he goes over Archie's message in his head.

What if Archie rings back and fires him? Does that mean he can't carry on with this job? No, no, he can't let that happen!

Biting his nails, he continues to ponder his options. Archie didn't actually use the words 'immediately'. *So...* he reasons, he could wait until he's got the charger. *But God!* W*hat a bloody pain in the arse this delivery is!* If it weren't for the fact that he had to wait in for it, he could pop out right now.

He thinks about the money he's being paid. He'll just have to wait, it's not as if Clarissa is asking much of him. He's reminded of the kitchen she asked him to clean. He'll go and do that now — it will keep his mind off things and hopefully the delivery will turn up soon.

As Malcolm makes his way to the kitchen, he thinks about his current conundrum. Before he'd started working, Malcolm had always attended his mum's medical appointments with her, but over the last month, since he's been working, Natalie the carer has gone instead. The consultant his mum went to see yesterday probably had some questions about something or other, quite possibly about her medication. Malcolm wasn't sure, and Archie hadn't said exactly what it was in his message — either way, the sooner he calls his mum the better. Archie also said to let him know that he'd got the message. Sighing, he takes his phone out to check the battery icon again. It's still showing one per cent. If he sends a text message now, his phone will more than likely die altogether. He doesn't want to risk it. Stuffing the phone back in his pocket, he makes his way to the kitchen.

Chapter 17
Room of Bones

'Now come along darling, we need to use the passageway to check the room and make sure everything is in order,' Clarissa says to Herbert. 'And please try not to get too excited, darling — you know what happened last year, and we can't afford to make another mistake.'

Herbert slides, eel-like down the bed post from where he's been sleeping on top of their four-poster bed.

'I need to check the locks aren't jammed up for a start, and I may have to do a bit of clearing up from last year,' she adds.

Clarissa walks over to the dressing table by the window and takes out a set of rusty keys from the top drawer. As she pads across the room, Herbert shadows her every step. Clarissa knows the minute the secret door to the passageway opens she'll have a hard time keeping him quiet.

She turns to him and presses a long red taloned finger to her lips.

'You must stay quiet, my darling,' she whispers, 'We can't frighten our guest. Stay close to me and don't make a sound.'

Herbert responds by flicking his forked tongue around his lips.

Smiling beatifically at him, she reaches out and presses a button set into the wooden panelling on the wall. There's a slight click and a hidden door creaks open, sending an icy draft of fetid air across the room.

Herbert immediately starts whining.

'Ssh, ssh! Please, you must be quiet,' Clarissa pleads.

Herbert lifts his claw-like hand and gently strokes her face, making a soft clacking sound with his pointed teeth.

'That's better, now come along,' She says as they make their way through to the secret corridor beyond the door.

The house was adapted by Herbert many decades ago. A secret set of passageways run around the circumference of the house and a staircase links the two floors at the back of the house. Herbert also crafted secret doors in every room, disguised within the wood panelling on the walls and almost invisible to the unsuspecting eye.

Making their way to the staircase, Herbert scurries along, sure-footed, despite the slimy water dripping from the walls and ceiling. His bright silver eyes full of mischief as they light the way for him. The cast iron spiral staircase leads directly to an antechamber below. Clarissa starts to make her way down, always barefoot when taking this route. Herbert is on all fours as he silently creeps down the curved handrail beside her. They reach the bottom of the staircase and Clarissa feels for the right key; after so many years, she knows exactly which key belongs to each door by touch alone.

The antechamber has three doors leading off it: one to the study, which is immediately in front of them, one to the right, which leads to the kitchen, and another door to their left. Clarissa places the key in the lock of the door to their left. It opens smoothly. The smell of decay immediately ripples through the open doorway, like an invisible tsunami wave, and Clarissa ushes Herbert inside, closing the door quickly behind them.

The entire room is full of human bones.

Bones of all sizes are strewn across the floor, the highest piles stacked up in the corners of the room like grotesque climbing frames.

'Oh Herbert!' Clarissa whispers, 'You know there hasn't been anything left in here to eat for the last few months. Why do you insist on coming in and messing it all up? You know how long it takes me to organise it all again.' Despite her words, Clarissa's voice is gentle; she knows very well that their one special meal a year no longer sustains them, particularly Herbert.

'Now you stay quiet, darling, whilst I make some room.'

Chapter 18
The Storm

Archie is sitting in the kitchen, scoffing a sandwich and scrolling through his messages on his phone. Still no response from Malcolm.

'Looks like that storm they predicted on the weather report this morning is closing in. Look how dark it's got outside,' Angie says over her shoulder as she rinses out dirty mugs in the sink.

'Hmm?' responds Archie, distracted.

'I said... look how dark the sky has gone already. You'd better go and check the shed — the door is virtually hanging off as it is, the last thing we need is the wind ripping it off and sending it hurtling through the kitchen window!'

Archie peeks out at the back garden. The blinds are pulled right up, but it's so dark outside it feels more like early evening, not lunchtime. The brooding sky looks ominous and branches on the trees are flailing wildly. He's not prone to superstition but he can't help feeling a sense of doom.

'Yeah, okay, love — I will, just let me check...' Archie pulls up the weather app for their part of South London.

'Yep, you're right,' he says, 'It's due to hit here about 2pm and go right through the night, almost til morning. I'm not happy about the party Evie's going to in Canehill tonight — in fact, I don't think she should go at all. They're warning people to stay indoors until it's over. I'd better go and have a word with her now.'

'Good luck with that. Rather you than me — you know she won't be happy. She'll probably sulk for a month,' she says, pulling an exaggerated grimace.

*

'You've got to be joking, Dad! This is so unfair; you can't be serious! Evie wails.

Despite Evie's predictable response, Archie tries to hide a half smile. Her last retort puts him in mind of the infamous tennis player, John McEnroe. And he knows from past experience that Evie's tantrums are just as legendary.

'Listen, Evie love,' he says placatingly, 'The weather report is advising everyone to stay indoors unless it's absolutely necessary to travel. Winds are going to be up to eighty miles an hour! I don't —'

'Dad, no! Please don't do this to me! You don't understand — you're ruining my life, why do you always do that? Everyone is expecting me. *Nobody else* has cancelled, and... and anyway, I can't cancel now, cos, like, Melanie said her mum is depending on *me* to help with the food and all that, so there's absolutely *no way* I can cancel.'

'Well, I'm happy to speak to her mum, I'm sure she'll understand–'

'You - are – joking - right?' Evie enunciates each word in disbelief. 'What, so, like, everyone in my class will know that you still treat me like I'm a bloody five-year-old? I even cleaned my room, just so you didn't have an excuse not to let me go, and now you're frightened I'll get killed by... by what? A bit of bloody wind? You're... you're so... fucking ridiculous!' she yells furiously as she flings her phone on to the bed.

'Evie, don't you dare swear at me like that! And don't raise your voice at me either. I'm your dad, I'm just worried about you, what if—'

'What? What exactly do you think will happen, Dad?' she shoots back. 'That Melanie's house will get blown down in a puff of wind and I'll end up under a pile of bricks? You're absolutely pathetic! It's just an excuse; you didn't want me to go in the first place, now you're just using this. You're *so transparent*, it's sad!' she yells in his face as she jumps up from the bed, heading for the door. She stomps past him, tears streaming down her face.

Archie hears the bathroom door slam — hard. Wincing, he raises his eyes to the ceiling. *God grant me patience.*

*

'Well, that went well,' Angie says as she turns to put the kettle on.

Archie slumps into a chair at the kitchen table.

'Look,' Angie presses, in an attempt to keep the peace. 'Why don't you agree to take her, and if it gets really bad out there, you can go and pick her up early, eh? I'm sure the other parents are having the same conversations with their kids as we are, and for all we know the party may well get cancelled anyway. In fact, I'm pretty sure it will, and that way you won't look like the bad guy.'

Chapter 19
Preparations

Malcolm can't believe how dark the house has got; its only late afternoon, but it looks more like midnight. Through the grimy kitchen window, ragged gunmetal grey clouds hang threateningly from a tar-black sky. The wind rattles at the decrepit windowpane. Its baleful howling sounds like someone is standing outside, whistling a mournful lullaby.

He hopes his mum isn't fretting about him. He pictures her now; she'll be asking Natalie to read out what's on TV tonight, weighing up which shows she'd prefer to see. He's sure Natalie will have managed to get his mum a cream cake, she seems like a decent carer. Malcolm has been buying his mum a cream cake every Saturday since he was a young boy. He first bought her one as a treat when he got his first pay for doing a paper round, and he's bought her one every week since. He really needs to call her. Absent-mindedly, he starts chewing his nails, silently admonishing the invisible delivery driver who, so far, has failed to turn up with the food. He went in search of Clarissa a while ago, but she's nowhere to be found and he doesn't feel confident enough to go knocking on bedroom doors to check if she's in any of them.

Checking the time on his phone, he sees it's four o'clock.

'Bugger it!' The battery icon is flashing which means it's about to die and he notices the text message icon is flashing too, indicating there's another text message. *God almighty!* He needs to get to the shops soon or they'll be closed — then he'll have to wait another day, and that won't bloody do.

He's already wiped down the counters and kitchen table. He'll start doing the drawers and cutlery next. He decides to give it until four-thirty. If the delivery hasn't turned up by then — sod it, he's going anyway.

Frustrated, he fills the sink with fresh water and starts emptying the first drawer. It's filled with knives of different sizes, some sharp and some blunt and rusty. There's even a big meat cleaver in there. It's absolutely filthy; with what looks like old rust covering even the handle. He checks the cupboard under the sink and finds some liquid detergent and a scourer. *That'll do.* He drops all the knives into the sink and leaves them to soak then sets about cleaning the cupboards. Malcolm doesn't mind cleaning, it gives him a chance to do something useful whilst daydreaming about a different type of life, one where his mum isn't ill and they live in a swanky house in absolute comfort.

Sweating profusely from all the vigorous scrubbing, Malcolm finally looks up from the sink, having cleaned nearly all of the drawers — there's just one more to do, but most of the more stubborn stains have come off and they're now laid out like soldiers standing to attention on the draining board. He can see through the window that the weather is really windy. Needing to cool down, he reaches up and pulls on the lever to open the window but it's stuck solid. He walks over to the back door and tries the handle, but that's locked too, he looks about for any sign of a key hook but there's nothing.

Tutting, he turns and starts to rifle through the last drawer: it's full of keys. There's an array of different keyrings. Some look like door keys, others look like car keys, one with a Ford leather key fob attached to it. Intrigued, he takes them all out and lays them on top of the kitchen counter. There are a few single keys in there, too. *God knows why people keep shit like this.* He can't quite imagine Clarissa driving, yet all these keys are testament to her past. They must have had several properties and cars for there to be so many of them.

Putting them back in the drawer, he catches sight of a bunch that looks much older than the rest. Picking them up, he notices the circular keyring has the letter 'M' in the middle of it with an arrow running straight across it. The design looks familiar, but he can't quite remember where he's seen it before. Holding it up towards the kitchen window to get a better look, he realises it's not an arrow, it's a serpent. *God, that's weird, but then this is a weird house and Clarissa is a weird person. I wonder if these are spare keys to the house ... He could go outside and check to see if he can get a signal on his phone in the back garden.*

Looking over his shoulder and cocking his ear to check Clarissa isn't clacking her way across the hallway, he takes the keys over to the back door. The first two keys don't even slide into the lock properly. He tries another and it slides in fully. Twisting it to the left, he feels a slight resistance, so he twists it harder. Then he hears a satisfying click.

It's obvious the door hasn't been opened in a long time — the lock is open, but it seems jammed. With a firm grip on the door handle, he pulls with all his strength. *Crack!* The door suddenly swings inwards, making him stumble backwards, and he loses his footing on the greasy lino, almost toppling to the floor. He lets out a loud grunt as he makes a grab for the kitchen counter, just managing to steady himself before nearly slipping on to his backside. His left hand starts to sting — he's grazed his knuckles on the counter edge and blood is oozing down his fingers. He grabs the cloth off the counter to wipe his hand, but as soon as he clears the blood it immediately starts to bleed again. *Damn it, I'll have to find a plaster now.*

Moving to the now open back door, he looks out at the large overgrown garden. The strength of the wind almost takes his breath away. He's never seen the weather so wild. The door starts banging against the worktop, so he grips the handle to steady it. He's just about to take his phone out of his back pocket when he hears a piercing scream floating on the wind — it sounds far away, yet nearby. Standing stock still, he tries to make out which direction it's coming from but it's hopeless with the wind coming at him from every direction. *Creepy. Must be the wind.* Shivering, he turns to go back inside, battling with the door to make sure it's securely closed against the gale that's trying to force its way into the house.

Just then, the grandfather clock in the hall chimes the half hour. *It must be half past four already.* He checks his phone. 'Shit! I don't believe it.' *It's not half past four, it's half past bloody five!'* 'Damn it to hell!' he roars. Distracted, he forgets to lock the back door and absently mindedly puts the keys into his pocket then goes back to the sink, thrusting his fists into the dirty sink water in frustration. He hangs his head and sighs. *Too bloody late now. That sodding delivery driver! And where the hell is Clarissa?* She knew he needed to go out.

He's furious; he got so carried away with cleaning and daydreaming about taking his mum to Ireland that he completely lost track of the time. He can feel his anger starting to build and his head starts to throb. 'You bloody idiot, Malcolm!'

He looks up through the kitchen window, trying to calm himself. Rain is now lashing at the pane, seemingly hellbent on breaking in, and the howling wind sounds like a quartet of banshees. The branches on the trees look like they're gesticulating furiously at him, as if in warning, reminding him of exhausted old men.

A thought suddenly hits him: *It's this bloody storm! Maybe that's why the driver hasn't turned up yet. God, what if he's had an accident?* Feeling slightly guilty now for wishing ill against the driver, his temper starts to recede. He's still really pissed off, though.

Chapter 20
Temptation

Clarissa has finished clearing a space on the floor in the room full of bones. Turning to Herbert, who's sat by the door waiting, she says, 'Now Herb—'

Herbert suddenly jerks his head up. He stands, sniffing the air. His body has gone rigid, like an animal on high alert. Then he throws his head back and lets out a spine-chilling scream.

Just then, Clarissa gets the same whiff of blood that has set Herbert off.

'Herbert! Herbert! Darling, please, ssh, ssh!' she pleads, teetering over to him with her arms outstretched in an attempt to settle him.

'That bloody idiot must have gone and done something to himself!' she cries. It's only the smell of blood that gets Herbert so agitated. That, and the taste of meat.

She's too slow, though — her arms meet thin air as Herbert's contorted frame jerks and skitters like lightning through the door and up the secret stairs.

She can hear a thud, thud, thud as Herbert makes his way around the house via the hidden passageway. She knows exactly where he's headed.

Hurrying out of the room, Clarissa goes to unlock the door that leads into the study. It's stiff because it hasn't been used in a few months, and although she's not as strong as Herbert, she has no problem opening it. She hurtles through the small room and out into the hallway. She can still hear Herbert's footsteps thumping across the house upstairs. He's so fast, she knows she has to reach the kitchen before he does, or their entire celebration will be at risk.

*

The kitchen is dark now, the sulphurous yellow glow from the ceiling light doing little to illuminate the room. There's an almighty crack of thunder; it sounds and feels like it's right on top of the house, followed by angry rumbling. Malcolm pauses, eyes directed up at the ceiling, listening. After a couple of seconds, another almighty crack. Then quiet. *God, it's getting worse, I'd better go and check the weather report on the TV.*

As he makes his way to the door, he hears footsteps thudding across the floor above the kitchen. They sound heavy and urgent, as if someone is running quickly from the back of the house to the front. *What the hell? That doesn't sound like thunder, or Clarissa.*

Suddenly, the kitchen door bangs open, making him jump.

Clarissa is standing there, looking dishevelled and flustered — a wild, desperate look in her eyes as she scans the room.

'Malcolm, there you are. Oh, thank...'

She appears relieved at the sight of him, and he wonders if the storm has frightened her.

'Oh, hello Clarissa. Actually, I was just coming to see if I could find you. The driver never turned up... and, well, I needed to go out? I, um, did say to you before. But, well, it's too late now, anyway.'

Clarissa doesn't move. She appears poised, listening for something.

'Are you alright? You look a bit...'

Then, as if she only just heard him, 'Driver? What driver? Have you seen someone?' she says, her voice rising, 'I mean... has...?'

Malcolm frowns. *She's seriously losing the plot.* 'No,' he says slowly, 'I haven't seen anyone yet, but I've been waiting.'

Clarissa looks blankly at him.

A subtle but exasperated expression crosses his face. 'You know — for the driver that's supposed to be delivering your food order?'

Clarissa continues to stare mutely at him.

'You said it was coming today,' he pushes on, a little irritated now. 'But it never turned up.' He shrugs his shoulders, consciously trying not to appear petulant, even though he's annoyed. 'Probably this bad weather and all that. But like I said, I was supposed to—'

'Oh, that! Yes, yes — of course, dear! Now I remember.'

From somewhere on the floor above comes the sound of scratching, followed by a low-pitched whine.

'What was that?' Malcolm asks, looking up. 'That didn't sound like thunder. Is that your husb—'

Clarissa laughs nervously. 'No, not at all, he's in bed. It's — it's just... the pipes!' she shouts, startling him a little.

Malcolm thinks she's definitely in a flap about something.

'Are you sure you're okay? You... you look a little bit funny, if you don't mind me saying — is it the storm that's bothering you? To be honest, I don't like them me self. In fact, I was just going to check the weather report—'

'No! Clarissa shrieks. 'Sorry, I just mean... it's not working. I think the aerial must have got damaged in the storm.'

'Well... that's okay, I can take a look at it if you want? The telly, that is?'

'No, really Malcolm, there's no need, but thank you anyway. We'll just have to make do for now.'

'But—'

A massive clap of thunder suddenly bellows angrily above the house, immediately followed by lightning that vividly lights up the kitchen, making them both look like X-ray silhouettes.

'Now,' Clarissa says, surveying the kitchen, 'You look like you've done a great job in here, Malcolm. Why don't you go to your room and have a little rest, dear? You must be tired. No need for you to be roaming around, no need at all.'

'Well… okay. But I don't have nothing else to do now until I have to serve your dinner later tonight… and, um, what about your delivery? Can you contact the supermarket to re-arrange it?'

He wonders if she has a mobile phone, and if she does, if she'd let him use it quickly. Somehow he doubts it, though.

'Supermarket,' she says, rolling the word around her mouth as though she's never spoken it before. 'No, don't worry dear, it's just a local man that comes. I'm sure he'll drop by tomorrow once the storm has passed.'

'Oh,' Malcolm says, disappointed.

Chapter 21
No Answer

'As storm Rebecca continues to wreak havoc across the south of England, people are being warned to stay indoors,' says the news presenter on the radio in Archie's kitchen. 'Gusts of wind in excess of eighty miles an hour have been battering the whole of the southeast coastline and, in the last hour, it's been confirmed by the Met Office that the storm is making its way inland. Power lines have already come down in many areas, leaving many families with no electricity.

'Our own weather reporter, Robert Kildare, has been seriously injured whilst out reporting on storm Rebecca in Canehill. He was taken to hospital with severe head injuries when a billboard was blown off the top of the Springtide shopping centre and fell on top of him. His injuries are not thought to be life threatening at the time of this report and he remains in a stable condition. We'll keep you updated.

'Meanwhile, the Government...'

Archie looks up at Angie, eyebrows raised. 'So, you still think we should let her go?'

'Look, love, we agreed,' says Angie. 'You told her she can go, after all. I'm certain the party will get cancelled, and when it does, she won't be able blame either of us. So just hang in there.'

'Okay,' Archie sighs. 'Actually, one of my carers, is on a private job over in Canehill. I was thinking that if I were to drop Evie off, I could pop in to check on him and—'

'Oh yeah, which carer? Mandy?' asks Angie.

'No, no, the new guy, Malcolm. You know, the odd one I told you about. Well, I had to speak to his mum yesterday as I was leaving the office. God, that was hard work,' he says, shaking his head. 'The old dear is almost completely deaf, and from what I could gather she needed to contact Malcolm — something to do with speaking to her doctor at the hospital. But guess what? When I checked his file, he'd only gone and left all his personal details blank! Can you bloody believe it?'

Angie shakes her head as she gets up and starts to take food out of the fridge in preparation for their dinner.

'I know, love,' she says, 'It's hard to get decent staff these days. Be careful though, Arch. You'd better make sure you get his personal details when you next speak to him. You can't afford to get into any more trouble with head office, not after they found out the last carer wasn't even allowed to work in the UK.'

'Yeah, you're right love. I'll try calling him again and if he doesn't answer, I'll call in on the way to the party.' Archie says as he reaches for his phone. He dials Malcolm's number but it rings out. He has a bad feeling that something is not right, but after the third attempt with no answer, he sighs and gives up.

'I'll try later,' he mutters.

Chapter 22
Time to Get Ready

'Right then,' says Clarissa, looking preoccupied. 'I have to go and sort out a few things. Why don't you go and have a rest, Malcolm? Maybe you'd like to have a shower, then you can relax a little. I'm sure you don't get much time to relax when you're at the care home, eh?'

Feeling offended, Malcolm frowns at Clarissa. He can't help showing his annoyance at her comment. He's not a child and doesn't like being told what to do. 'A shower?' he says huffily.

Clarissa immediately sees she's overstepped the mark. 'What I mean, dear, is... Well — your manager told me how hard you work,' she says, 'and I just thought you'd appreciate some time to relax. You're only here for a short while, and you may as well make the most of it, that's all. I would have asked you to do some work in the garden, but what with the storm and everything... Of course, I could find some other work for you to do — if you really want to — but I just thought...' she trails off, waiting for her words to sink in.

Malcolm now feels guilty for his kneejerk reaction — she's only trying to be kind to him, and he doesn't particularly want to do any more work if he can help it. He's pleased that Archie has noticed how hard he works, between his day job and looking after his mum in the evenings, he's nearly always exhausted.

'Well... I s'pose if you don't need me for anything then I'll take a shower and maybe get a bit of shut eye.'

'Excellent,' she says, scanning the kitchen again before making her way out.

Malcolm waits for the door to close then feels for the bunch of keys in his back pocket. He knows he should put them back, really. He's no right to have the keys to the house, if that is in fact what they are. But he doesn't like the idea that the doors to the house are kept locked and he can't leave if he needs to. Unlikely, but what if there were a fire?'

*

Clarissa scuttles across the hall and into the study. No sign of Herbert, thankfully. He must have gone back to their bedroom. Entering the study, she goes over to the secret door by the bookcase — it's only slightly ajar and it's doubtful that imbecile Malcolm would have noticed it, but at this stage she can't take any risks. She's just about to step through the door

106

when she has a thought. She steps back over to the TV. There are two leads coming out of the back of the set: the main power plug and the aerial. She pulls the aerial out and tucks it under the edge of the carpet, satisfied that even if Malcolm does come in here, he'll think the TV isn't working because of the storm.

As she steps through into the antechamber, she immediately sees Herbert lurking outside the secret door to the kitchen. Hurrying over to him, she inadvertently forgets to lock the door behind her.

'Herbert! Come away, darling,' she whispers urgently, holding out her hand to him. Herbert is concentrating so hard on smelling what lies beyond in the kitchen that she makes him jump. Realising he's been caught out, he skulks towards her and takes her hand.

'Come, darling,' she says, 'It's no good spying on him, it won't be long now.' Her heart could break for him because she knows how hungry he is.

*

Clarissa and Herbert lie side-by-side on their king size bed. Herbert has finally settled down, but she knows from the way his body is convulsing every few minutes that he's suffering from lack of food.

Speaking in their native tongue, Clarissa says, 'Everything is nearly ready. You know what we have to do, and there can be no mistakes this time, darling. It was far too messy last year. You must wait until the thirteenth chime; only then can you take him, alright, my love?'

Herbert lets out a deep and hideous gurgling sound — his energy is fading fast — but Clarissa knows when the time comes, nothing will hold him back.

As Herbert's silver eyes starts to close in slumber, Clarissa gets up and starts to get ready. Her gown and her walking stick are already laid out on the armchair. She sits at the dressing table, doing her make up, and reflects on all the years they have performed this ritual. It should be perfected by now, yet each year, with so many variables, there's always room for something to go wrong. But she's adamant this year everything will go off without a hitch. She reminds herself to ensure the secret doors to the kitchen and bone room are unlocked so they can be accessed quickly. She smiles at her reflection when she thinks about Malcolm; yes, she made a good choice this year. The imbecile has already cleaned all the equipment they'll need.

After applying her make-up, she appraises herself in the mirror; beautiful. Her long white hair looks like tendrils of liquid pearl as it ripples down her back. Her lips, a luscious scarlet, match the colour of her gown, which has the Meyers' family crest of the serpent delicately stitched along the neckline in silver thread. Her skin is so white she appears almost translucent. When she has to go into the *outside* world, she knows how different she appears to other people; haggard, old and weak. Only Herbert has the ability to see her as she really is — the real her — that's part of the magic of what they are.

Rising from the chair, she picks up her walking stick, the head of which is fashioned into the head of a serpent. It pulsates under her touch — a beautiful gift, hand-carved by her beloved Herbert over a century ago.

Chapter 23
The Book

Malcolm can barely see himself in the bathroom mirror. The overhead light is on, but the feeble light does little to penetrate the darkness of the raging storm outside. The rain is battering every part of the house and hammering loudly on the bathroom window. It feels almost personal with its persistent and spiteful drumbeat. Even the wind feels like it's in cahoots with the rain — a double act, roaring fiercely as it bellows a thunderous, haunting symphony.

Having showered in what he can only describe as a trickle of lukewarm water, he stands, assessing the stubble on his face, which is itching badly. He knows he should have shaved this morning, but he couldn't be bothered. Assessing the state of his now mainly silver bristles, he thinks of his mum — she would poke fun at the sight of him, but in a loving way. *She'd* never tell him when to take a shower. His stomach lurches with anxiety — she'll be worried about him; he hasn't seen her since Thursday night. Today was a disaster, having to

111

wait in all day for a delivery that never materialised. He decides to check the battery on his phone after his shower. He just might be able to give her a quick call before she goes to bed. Picking up his razor, he dips it into the tepid water and starts to shave.

*

A clap of thunder wakes Malcolm. It feels late and the room is shrouded in darkness. Disoriented and worried about the time, he lurches across the room, blindly groping for the light switch by the door. Nothing. 'Shit.' He can feel panic rising in his chest and wonders if there has been a power cut. He flicks the switch again. The lightbulb flickers on and off a couple of times, then thankfully stays on. He goes over to the bedside table and switches on his phone. It's still showing no signal with one per cent battery.

He hadn't intended on falling asleep, but he feels refreshed, realising he must have been more tired than he thought after the previous night's disturbed sleep. Plonking down on the bed, he wonders what to do with himself. He still has a little time to kill before serving the food. Maybe he should call his mum now? *No, it's late — I'd rather wait until tomorrow and see if I can get a signal in the garden. Yep, that's what I'll do, I'll call her once I've charged the phone.* Still feeling irked that the TV isn't working, he decides to go downstairs to take a look at it anyway.

There's no overhead light on in the landing, which unnerves him, so he reaches for the light switch. But despite him flicking it up and down several times, the light doesn't come on. He sees a faint light coming from below, so as quietly as he can, he makes his way downstairs.

Relieved the light is working in the study, he gently closes the door behind him, then plods over to the TV and turns it on. It crackles but there's no picture, just a grainy white and grey background. 'Damn it'. He gives it a bang, just for good measure, then plops himself down on the armchair. *This is gonna be a long week,* he thinks as he scans the room, looking for something to do. He sees there are all sorts of curious pictures hanging on the walls that he hadn't noticed before, but his eyes settle on the bookshelves and the book he was looking at the day before. Something like defiance overcomes him and guiltily, he skulks over to the shelf. *What else am I supposed to do? I can't just sit for hours on end doing nothing all week.*

As he reaches out to take the book off the shelf, he feels a slight draft coming from his left. Turning to check where it's coming from, he gets a whiff of something awful. He's surprised as he spies the little door he thought was bricked up is slightly ajar now. *Hmm... must be some sort of storage space.* As his hand reaches out to push it open further, he suddenly hears Clarissa's heels tapping across the floor outside the study. He freezes. *Shit*! He doesn't fancy getting caught in here by the bookcase again, but her footsteps pass the study door. Breathing a sigh of relief, he turns back to the bookshelf. *Incubus – Succubus* by H. Meyer. Feeling like a real thief, he stuffs it up his jumper as quickly as he can. If Clarissa walked in now, he'd feel not only humiliated at being caught, but worse than that, he realises he'd be terrified of her reaction. He couldn't stand to witness her throwing another hissy fit like the last time; she'd really frightened him. Just thinking about the way she looked sometimes made his flesh crawl. He couldn't help feeling there was something unnatural about her and this house, but he couldn't quite put his finger on it.

Tiptoeing across the room, he cocks his ear to the door: silence. Clarissa must have gone into the kitchen for something. He'll have to be quick. Putting his hand on the doorknob, he turns it gently and peeps out into the hallway while gradually opening the door. The coast is clear. Hunching his shoulders, he creeps as quickly and as quietly as he can across the hall, up the stairs and into his bedroom.

Once inside, he wipes his brow and sits down on the edge of the bed, the heavy book in his lap. The faint overhead light doesn't throw out much light, but it's just enough for him to read.

Propping the pillows up against the headboard, he heaves his legs up on to the bed and makes himself comfortable.

The first thing he notices about the book is how old it feels, and there's a funny smell coming off the pages as he flicks through them. Awkwardly, he holds it up to his nose, immediately regretting it as he recoils from the putrid, animalistic smell. The pages don't even feel like paper — something much thicker, but he's not sure what. The book cover is black and undoubtedly leather; it's cracked all over and reminds him of the deep fissures of an ancient tree trunk, like the ones in his local park. There's a picture of a serpent with its jaws wide open and strange silver symbols arranged around the edges. He's just about to open it when he notices something else — within the serpent's mouth is the letter 'M' in gold. He lets out a gasp and chucks the book down beside him. Reaching into his back pocket, he pulls out the bunch of keys he found in the kitchen drawer. 'Well, I'll be damned,' he whispers.

Malcolm closes the book and sits up abruptly, having read all the pages, his mind is now racing. He can't quite believe what he's just read. Spitting out a piece of chewed nail, he tries to read the last page again, but it's no use — no matter how hard he tries to concentrate on the words, they're just swimming on the page, as if they're being tumbled about like the leaves in the storm outside. His thoughts clatter around his mind chaotically, in an attempt to piece everything together. Then, finally, realisation hits.

He swings his legs off the bed on to the floor with a thud. He knows he needs to concentrate. 'Think, Malcolm, think!' he says as he cups his head in his hands.

The book is unlike any other book he's ever read before. It's handwritten and takes the form of a manual. The first couple of pages talk about the ancestry of the Meyer family, which goes back hundreds and hundreds of years. There's a crude picture of the family crest, which he recognises now as the same as the design on the keyring, which he's acutely aware of in his back pocket. Subsequent pages go on to tell of 'The Taking Ritual', which takes place at the same time every year on 21st March and is followed by a great feast and celebration.

A '*live fayre*' must come willingly to the abode where the ritual takes place.

The *live fayre* must be of clean skin and must also clean the blade that will take its life.

And finally, the *live fayre* cannot be cut until the clock strikes the thirteenth hour — only then will the blood, bone, and flesh of the *live fayre* be pure enough to sustain the Incubus and Succubus for another year.

If only he knew what an incubus and succubus were. He's never heard the terms before now, but whatever they are, he doesn't like the sound of them. Frowning deeply, he tries to make sense of it. *The thirteenth hour? Well, that's nonsense for a start,* he thinks. *And fayre? Hang on, doesn't that mean food? How the hell can food clean its own...*

'Oh my God — live food!' Malcolm shrieks as he jumps up. 'What the...?'
No, no, you idiot, Malcolm, calm down! That's a mad idea. It must mean some kind of live animal. A pig, maybe? But how would a pig clean its own blade?

Malcolm thrusts the book on to the bed in disgust, just as the overhead light starts flickering. He looks up, willing it to stay on. *Please,* he silently begs. *I can't be in darkness now.*

Images from the last two days start slotting together in his mind like a giant jigsaw. The 'M' crested keyring has to be connected to Clarissa and her husband, who have the same surname, Meyer. The author, H Meyer, of course couldn't possibly be Herbert — *that would make him over five-hundred years old! No, that's a silly idea* — but there's no doubt in Malcolm's mind that it was probably written by one of Herbert's ancestors.

Then there's that awful dining table with the iron rings on it. That must be used to hold the poor live animal down. He shudders. *But surely the book is just a work of fiction? Old tales and even nursery rhymes are really gruesome.* Just

117

then, an image of Little Red Riding Hood being eaten by a wolf pops into his mind. He sweeps the thought away and tries to rationalise. *It's just a book*, he tells himself. But his gut is telling him something is not quite right. This whole bloody job is not quite right. His dear mum always told him to follow his gut, and something has felt off kilter ever since he arrived at this creepy house. *I really want to leave — I'll just have to find another way to get the money I need for mum.*

It's late. Malcolm has got so carried away reading the book that he's lost track of time. *Still*, he thinks, if he's quick, he just has time to sneak into the study and return the book before serving Clarissa's food. After that, he'll pack his things and get out of here — storm or no storm, he's not staying in this house a second longer than he has to.

Grabbing the book, he makes his way out of the room. As he tries to creep quietly down the dimly lit staircase, he hears a loud bang that he thinks comes from the direction of the kitchen. It sounds like wood cracking. He stops dead still, poised mid-step, holding his breath and listening intently, but all he can hear is the wind howling outside, then an almighty clap of thunder. His stomach lurches with a bolt of fear, he clasps it, hoping to stop the sensation of eels wriggling in his belly. He can't decide what to do; go straight to the study and return the book or go and investigate the noise.

Chapter 24
Taxi Service

'Honestly, I really don't mind,' says Melanie's mum. 'It's all arranged. I'm picking up the girls and Melanie's dad is picking up the boys, it should be—'

'No, really,' Archie interjects, 'I'm happy to—'

'Nonsense! We wouldn't hear of it, would we Mark?' Melanie's mum calls to someone Archie can't see but can hear blathering on to someone else in the background.

'Look,' continues Melanie's mum. 'I know we can all get a bit precious with our daughters, but I promise you — they'll be absolutely fine. I'll guard them with my life! You dads, honestly, you're all the same about your baby girls. Well, they're fifteen now! They know more than we ever did at that age, and don't tell me you don't remember what it was like being fifteen?'

Archie can't stand her patronising tone. Grinding his teeth helps to keep him from saying what he really feels like saying, which is: *Who the hell do you think you are, telling me how to parent my own daughter?* Instead, he takes a deep breath, 'Okay, well, if you're sure then. I'll be there to collect her at 12.30, but *please* call me if the weather gets worse and you need me to collect her earlier. You have my number.'

'Sure, no problem and I'm glad you don't mind Evie staying on for half an hour or so after the party with a few of the others to help clear up. I think it's a good thing, don't you? I think it's good to teach them about responsibility and all that.'

'Okay,' Archie sighs resignedly, 'I'll see you later.'

'Can you believe it?' Archie shouts to Angie, who's watching TV in the living room next door. 'God almighty! Parents like that should be bloody strung up. Not only are they going ahead with the party in this weather, but she had the bare faced cheek to more or less imply I was molly coddling Evie! Bloody cheek!' Archie says as he makes his way over to a drawer and starts rifling through it, searching for his emergency pack of cigarettes. Feeling justified for breaking a two-week run of not smoking, but still annoyed at himself because he just couldn't seem to quit for longer than a few weeks at a time.

'Pour me a wine while you're in there love, would you?' Angie calls back. Archie gets a glass down from a cupboard and, as he takes out the chilled white wine from the fridge, he spies his beers. Pouring the wine, he still feels irked at Melanie's mum's comments. *Irresponsible parenting, the world's full of it! No wonder our kids have gone off the bloody rails*. He pulls out a bottle of cold beer — absolutely no reason now why he can't have one, seeing as he won't be driving until much later tonight.

Archie puts the wine glass down on the coffee table along with his beer.

'So, what's the latest?' asks Angie as she picks up her wine and takes a big gulp.

'Well, Melanie's mum is picking Evie up at seven-thirty, then I'll collect her at twelve-thirty. Apparently the party has to finish by midnight, as they can't have the music on after that. Something to do with the law. It's considered anti-social... I think. Anyway, it's later than I'd like, but it is what it is. So much for it being cancelled!' He looks accusingly at Angie.

'Don't blame me! You thought as well as I did it would get cancelled!' Angie counters. 'Look, love, try not to worry too much. She's fifteen, this is one of many parties she'll be going to. Trust me, I'm sure she'll be absolutely fine.'

'Yeah, I suppose. I just hope there's no alcohol. You know what they're like at that age.

'Yes, I certainly do!' she says as she smiles at him 'And *you* certainly drank at fifteen!'

Archie flings a cushion at her. 'By the way,' he says, lighting up a cigarette, 'I think I'll drop in to that client's house I was telling you about. It's on the way, so I'll pop in when I drive

121

over to collect Evie later — you know, the one where Malcolm's on a job.'

'Okay, but won't it be a bit late? What will he think, you turning up at that hour?'

'Thing is, I've been calling him all day and he's not answering. I just want to make sure everything is alright... He's just a bit... I don't know — innocent? He kind of reminds me of a boy I used to know at school who always got bullied; the thing is, I always *wanted* to help him out, but you know what it's like, I never actually did and... well it didn't turn out too well for him in the end and I don't know... I guess part of me wishes I'd done something to help him. If he'd gone to work for any other client then fine, but that woman he's gone to work for... well, she's a bit... odd to say the least. I don't know why, but I just feel something isn't right and I want to make sure he calls his mum.'

'Well, you know best, but I still think it'll be a bit late; won't they be in bed at that time of night?'

'Yeah, you might be right, love, but if either Malcolm or the old bat complain about it, I'll say the fact that he's not answering his phone when I need to contact him urgently about a family matter, gives me the right as his manager to make sure everything is alright. After all what if his mother had been admitted to hospital? No, I know it'll be late but I feel it's the right thing to do.'

*

Archie checks the time on his dashboard clock: eleven-fifteen pm. Plenty of time to pop in to check in on Malcolm before he collects Evie. His satnav is telling him his estimated arrival to Angel Road is in twelve minutes. He decided earlier, he doesn't care about the time, Malcolm should have answered his bloody phone. It isn't just that, though; a bad feeling had been needling him all day and the phone call he'd had with Malcom's mum yesterday hadn't helped and was still playing on his mind.

The wipers are virtually useless against the rain that's pouring down his windscreen like a river. This will be a slow drive. Shaking his head, he sighs, annoyed at himself for letting Evie go to a party in this weather. He should have put his foot down, he thinks, as he sees yet another large tree branch strewn across the grass verge. The storm has really gained momentum over the last couple of hours. He feels as if he's in the middle of a monsoon. He can't ever remember seeing so much forked lightning illuminating the sky. It feels almost biblical.

Archie slows the car to a crawl as the satnav announces, 'You will reach your destination in one minute.' The rainwater is cascading relentlessly down the road and into the gutters, which are already overflowing.

'You have reached your destination,' the satnav informs him. He pulls over to the curb and kills the engine. He opens his side window and chucks his cigarette butt on to the pavement, then peers through the pouring rain at The Manse. He can't see much beyond the big black gates, but he makes out what looks like a fair-sized house set quite far back from the road with a long snaking path leading up to the front door. There's no sign of life and the house is completely dark.

'Maybe they're all in bed after all,' he mutters, considering what to do next. Then he pulls out his phone. He dials Malcolm's number, but as he expected, it goes straight to voicemail. 'Sod this.' he says. And, zipping up the front of his parka and pulling his hood over his head, he opens his car door.

Archie pulls the bell rope at the side of the gate, hopping from one foot to another, trying to keep warm as he waits. Nothing happens — the gates remain firmly closed. Rain streaks down his face, almost blinding him as he peers at the house beyond the iron gates. Now he's a bit closer, he can see a few dim lights behind the windows in a couple of the rooms downstairs. *There must be a way in,* he thinks, scanning the rest of the garden, but the property appears to be surrounded by a tall brick wall. As he continues to look around, he spies a side gate that's built into the left-hand side of the wall. His line of vision follows the perimeter of the property. 'Bingo!' he says as he notices a narrow alleyway alongside the wall, which must lead up to the side gate. He starts walking and hopes the gate is open.

Chapter 25
The Thirteenth Hour

Malcolm decides to put the book back first, then go to the kitchen to investigate the noise. If Clarissa is in the kitchen, he doesn't want her to see that he's got it.

In the study, he gently slides the book back on to the shelf, noticing the small door beside the bookcase is still ajar. He hasn't got time to investigate it now, so he makes his way across the hall towards the kitchen. A thought occurs to him and, swivelling on his heel, he changes direction and walks over to the grandfather clock that stands opposite the study door. He starts counting the roman numerals on the clock face. His jaw drops.

'Oh my God, I don't believe it,' he says, backing away. He trots back to the study, retrieves the book and walks towards the kitchen when suddenly the house is plunged into darkness.

'Shit!' he cries, spinning around blindly. *Don't panic — it must be a power cut, that's all.* Despite telling himself that, he starts hyperventilating. His heart thumps in his chest and almost up into his throat.

He hates the dark; has done ever since he was a child. He tries to stay calm and regulate his breathing, taking a deep breath in, then blowing it out again slowly. That's what his mum used to tell him to do when he was young, having one of his frequent panic attacks. 'That's it, love,' she'd say calmly, 'Focus on your breathing: in... out... in... out'...' But it's not working now — no matter how hard he tries, he can't concentrate. As he wipes the sweat trickling down the back of his neck, all he can think about is the fact he counted thirteen numbers on the clock face and what the book stated will happen at the strike of the Thirteenth Hour.

I'll grab my stuff now and go. His breathing slows a little as his eyes start to adjust to the dark and he realises he's facing the front door.

He's just about to reach out to check if the door is unlocked when he hears the kitchen door behind him creak open slowly. His body goes rigid with fear, he turns and squints through the darkness, ears pricked. He can't see anything and there's nothing but silence — no rain, no thunder, just utter silence. His mind is racing. His eyes dart around the hall, checking for any moving shapes, but he can barely see anything. Suddenly, he hears heavy breathing right in front of him. His entire body jerks as a wave of terror courses through him and he lets out a scream.

Blindly, he turns and lurches towards what he hopes is the front door, arms outstretched — half running, half tripping over his own feet. *I've got to get out. I must get out of this house.*

But just as his fingers are within touching distance of it, a hand grabs his shoulder.

'Argh! Get away from me — you... you mad bitch!' He turns and raises the book ready to strike.

'Malcolm! Malcolm! Calm down, it's okay — it's me, Archie.'

Malcolm spins towards the voice, eyes wide in disbelief, trembling all over as his brain tries to understand what's going on, but he can't make sense of anything.

'What the... Archie...? What the bloody hell is going on? Why are you here? Why are you trying to frighten the life out of me? You bastard!' he shrieks at the dark shadow that is Archie.

Malcolm backs away until he juts up against the front door. He raises his arm again, still clutching the heavy book as a weapon. He feels his arm start to tremble at the effort of holding it aloft and his fingers cramp up from holding it so tightly.

'Don't touch me!' Malcolm shouts at the shadow in front of him, turning to make a last attempt at scrabbling for the door handle, but he can't remember which side of the door it's on.

'Malcolm, please stop yelling, it's okay, I just came to check everything was alright. There's a power cut—'

'I don't care! I have to get out of here… I'm leaving right now!' he shouts, 'There's bloody iron rings on the dining table and… and that clock — it says thirteen, see? The same as this disgusting book!' He flings the book onto the floor. He can't stand to touch it a second longer. 'I'm going right now—'

'Fine, Malcolm,' Archie says, putting his hands up in a gesture of surrender. 'It's not a problem — I'll take you home myself, I promise, just please try and stay calm.'

Malcolm flinches, still not trusting what's going on. *What if Archie is in on this with Clarissa?'*

Archie lets his hands drop to his sides. 'C'mon,' he says, gently. 'I've got the car outside. Do you need to get anything before we leave, or—'

Just then, there's a crashing sound from somewhere upstairs. It doesn't sound like thunder.

'Quick, it's her! We've got to get out of here,' Malcolm says in a strangled voice.

'What the hell?' Archie whispers. 'What do you mean? Are you talking about Clari—'

130

Malcolm has already turned on his heel and, finding the door handle at last, starts yanking on it, but it's locked. 'Shit, shit, shit!' he spits in frustration. Twirling frantically, he bangs straight into Archie's chest.

'Oof!' Archie wheezes as Malcolm's body hits him.

'Shh!' Malcolm gasps. Then, urgently, 'Quick, go the other way — through the kitchen, there's a back door, it should be open. Hurry, hurry!'

'Hang on, let me switch my phone torch on.'

As they look at each other in the semi darkness, an unspoken agreement passes between them, and they start to make their way across the hall to the kitchen. But two things happen at once. They both jump as the grandfather clock strikes midnight, and then a tall, white figure jumps sideways from the top of the staircase, landing right in front of the kitchen door, blocking their path.

Malcolm shrieks.

Archie stands rigid in shock.

The tall, white male figure doesn't move. It's staring straight at them, its piercing silver eyes glowering at them through the shadowy light. As it slowly opens its mouth, the torch light from the phone reveals shiny black pointed teeth as crystal white saliva drips copiously onto the floor, then suddenly it lets out demonic scream.

'What the fu…?' The words die on Archie's lips as the figure starts to walk slowly towards them.

Malcolm whimpers, then grabs Archie's arm. 'This way, quick!'

They turn as one, Malcolm's hand firm on Archie's arm as he drags him to the study. They charge through the study door, then turn and press their weight against it.

'We can't stay like this! Get something to block it, quickly,' Archie orders through ragged breaths.

Malcolm doesn't waste any time. He grabs hold of the armchair, dragging it back to the door where Archie is stood, bracing his shoulder against it.

Archie drops his shoulder and together they heave the armchair up underneath the door handle. Malcolm realises with alarm that if that… thing, that… creature is intent on getting in, then a chair is probably not going to cut it. After all — he's just witnessed it leap from the top of the staircase without so much as a scratch.

Archie scans the dark room desperately before turning to Malcolm. 'What the hell was that thing?'

Malcolm stands frozen, staring at the door. 'I knew something wasn't bloody right. Just my bloody luck!' he whimpers. 'It's all there in that terrible book. I think they want to kill me —

us!' he blurts, then starts gibbering about live fayre and the number thirteen.

'I don't know what you're on about! You're not making any sense. Listen to me, Malcolm — how do we get out of here?' Archie says, panic now in his voice.

Malcolm is becoming more and more incoherent as he continues talking gibberish. 'The keyring… and, you know… the name Meyers? It all makes sense — well it must be his grandad or something that wrote it… but they… have a keyring and the name Meyers and there are iron rings on…'

The grandfather clock in the hall starts chiming again.

Malcolm suddenly stops talking. Then, his voice rising to a shriek, 'Oh my God — thirteen! It's gonna strike thirteen! It's gonna kill us!' Malcom clasps his hands over his ears and starts wailing loudly.

Archie grabs Malcolm by the shoulders, shaking him roughly. 'For God's sake, Malcolm! Get a grip, calm down, and tell me what the hell you're talking about!'

'It's all in the book I found. Clarissa must be a devil! And… when it strikes thirteen, she's gonna kill us! She's deran—'

Bang. The study door shakes on its hinges.

'Fuck!' says Archie. 'Right, I understand you're scared Malcolm, but we have to get out of this room — now!' He scans the study again. 'What can we use to keep that thing out? I need to call the police...' His words are drowned out by another bang, even louder this time, accompanied by the brutal sound of the wooden door cracking.

Hands shaking, Archie grabs his phone out of his coat pocket and starts dialling.

Another almighty bang on the door makes them both jump wildly. This time it sounds like the door is going to come crashing down.

'Argh!' Malcolm reaches out to grab Archie's arm, shouting, 'Quick, quick — the little door, the little door!' As Malcolm turns to run towards the bookcase, he accidently knocks the phone out of Archie's hand. It skitters off somewhere across the room, its illuminated screen bouncing up and down in the darkness.

'Shit! You idi—'

The study door suddenly comes crashing in, showering them both in wooden splinters.

Malcolm yells out as he grabs Archie's coat and drags him backwards towards the bookshelf, his other hand outstretched, searching for the small secret door. Relief washes over him as he finds it. 'Thank God, it's still open,' Malcolm says. 'In here — quick, bend down and follow me.' Malcolm scrambles as fast as he can through the small door, banging his shoulders painfully as he thrusts his body forward, but he doesn't feel the pain — only a sense of urgency and terror — his only thought is to get away from that *thing*. He hears Archie's heavy breathing and grunting close behind him. As soon as he's through, he turns, offering his hand to Archie, who grasps it. Malcolm tightens his grip and pulls, but something isn't right. Archie seems to be pulling the opposite way. *What the....?*

'Malcolm — help! It's got my leg!' Archie cries.

'No — no, hang on,' Malcolm gasps, trying to hold onto him. Malcolm brings his knees up, putting one foot either side of the door, trying to keep hold of Archie's hand, but his sweaty palm is making it difficult and Archie's hand starts slipping. *There's nothing for it,* he thinks. He lets go momentarily, then quickly grabs both cuffs of Archie's coat. He tightens his grip with both hands and heaves Archie towards him with all his strength.

'Malcolm, please! Pull... harder — it won't let go of my legs!'

Malcolm groans as he pulls as hard as he can on Archie's coat cuffs. Sweat trickles off his forehead into his eyes but he's gaining traction now; he can feel Archie starting to slide towards him. Suddenly, there's no resistance, and Malcolm's arms fling backwards, hitting him straight in the face. He's left holding nothing but the coat.

Malcolm stares at the now empty black space beyond and into the study through the open secret door. There's nothing there but darkness. He grabs the door handle and pulls it shut, then scuttles backwards on his bum until his body hits something hard. He sits there, dumbfounded, staring wide-eyed at the door. *This can't be happening!* He's only vaguely aware of the tears running down his face.

Stunned, Malcolm can't believe what happened in the space of a few seconds. But it must have, because… *Archie is… gone. That… that thing has taken him. Oh my god, oh my god.* He starts hyperventilating again. *I must be dreaming — yes, that's it. This is just another nightmare, Malcolm — wake up!*

The grandfather clock chimes again, bringing him out of his fugue. 'No, this isn't a dream,' he whispers, feeling Archie's coat in his hands. He's got no idea if that last chime was the thirteenth and he's got no intention of finding out; he only knows he must get out of here alive.

Malcolm pulls his knees up to his chest, shaking and clutching Archie's coat like a talisman, looking around the dark space. He can sense it's bigger than he imagined; there are two dark shapes either side of him that look like doors. Shakily, he stands, one hand exploring the solid thing behind him — it feels like some sort of railing. He puts Archie's coat on the floor at his feet and lets his hands roam, all the while hoping to God that the creature isn't sitting there waiting to grab him. After feeling as much as he dares, he realises he's at the bottom of a staircase.

Anxiety rips through his gut as he tries to think what to do. *Shall I go up the stairs? Or should I try and get Archie's phone from the study? But what if that thing is still in there, waiting for me?* Sweat breaks out on his forehead as he silently curses himself for leaving his own phone in the bedroom upstairs. If he had it with him now, he could have called the police. *Shit, no that wouldn't work, cos there's no signal on his phone in this house. Shit, shit. What to do? But what if he could get a signal from the garden? Maybe he could fetch his phone and try and make it through the back door?* Mentally, he tries to picture where the back stairs might lead to in the house. He knows he's behind the study, which means he's on the *opposite* side to his bedroom. He doesn't fancy his chances. *No. I'll check the two doors down here first, maybe one of them leads outside.*

He bends down to pick up Archie's coat, when something metallic clatters to the floor. Frowning, he gets down on his knees and starts feeling around the floor until his hand lands on something small and oblong. It's a lighter. Stuffing it in his back pocket, he stands — his knees crack with the effort and he lets out a groan. He looks to the door on his left and, for some bizarre reason he doesn't understand, he puts Archie's coat on. *Here goes,* he thinks, bracing himself.

Holding his breath, he opens the door as slowly as he can, grateful that it doesn't make any sound. His guts are still twisting painfully at the thought of that creature lurking in wait for him, but all he can think of is finding Archie and getting out of here and home to his mum. He's hoping this room will lead to a way out. He feels sweat trickling down the back of his neck as he opens the door fully and breathes a sigh of relief when nothing springs out at him. 'Thank God,' he whispers. Reaching into his back pocket, he pulls out the lighter. Taking a final tentative step into the room, he flicks it on and a tiny flame erupts from his hand. The flame doesn't throw out much light, and all he can make out is... *sticks*? They're strewn everywhere. Great piles of them are heaped randomly all over — they're even piled up against the corners of the room. He steps over to the nearest pile, holding the lighter as steady as he can, so the flame doesn't go out, and reaches down with his other hand to pick one up. He's just about to touch it when his hand stops midway.

'Oh my God!' he cries as he realises it's not a stick — it's a human leg bone. Jerking upright, he looks around the room, eyes agog, the flame from the lighter casting eerie shadows on the walls as it waves wildly in his trembling hand.

There's no doubt in his mind; he knows what they are. He stares dumbfounded at the piles all around him, he sees a human skull and what looks like a ribcage and even a hand. Suddenly, he can't breathe. He puts a hand to his chest as his heart pumps madly and he struggles to get air into his lungs, thinking any second he's going to be sick — or worse, have a heart attack.

Panic-driven now, he swivels towards the door and thinks he hears a distant whispering voice. It sounds female. *Clarissa!* Taking his finger off the lighter, he strains every one of his senses trying to *feel* what direction the voice came from, but he can't hear anything. Silently, he creeps through the open door, hoping to God that he's not walking straight towards her. He stops when he reaches the bottom of the staircase.

He hears it again. *That's definitely Clarissa's voice whispering to someone. It came from the top of the stairs.*

'Why did that idiot have to come here and ruin everything? What a disaster! I can't believe it — just when everything was going so well,' Clarissa hisses. 'But don't worry, darling, we'll just have to get rid of the manager later. It won't be easy, but we have no choice. Now come, our meal must be taken and soon, before the thirteenth hour ends. I think he's hiding somewhere downstairs.'

That's what you think, you bitch! Malcolm thinks, as an image of Archie flashes through his mind. *You can try all you like, but you sure as hell won't kill me.*

Chapter 26
Mission Impossible

Archie's eyes flutter awake. He immediately feels a searing pain shooting up his right leg, and his head feels like it's been bashed in with a hammer. 'Agh. What the...? Where...?' He moans groggily, trying to focus on his surroundings, but everything is blurry and he realises it's because he's not wearing his glasses.

Renewed terror courses through him as he remembers the creature grabbing hold of his leg as he tried to escape. It dragged him to the top of stairs, his head ricocheting off each step before they got to the top. The creature's strength was supernatural and Archie had felt like an inconsequential ragdoll. Once they'd reached the landing, the creature had opened a door on the right, yanked Archie up by his ankle, looked him straight in the eye and slung him across the room like a petulant child. Archie's body had smashed against the far wall, and that was the last thing he remembered before passing out.

I've got to get out of here. Tentatively, he pats the floor around him, searching for his glasses. They didn't fall far. His hand lands on them a couple of inches away, and thankfully they're still in one piece. Putting them on quickly, he sits up and looks around. It's a large dark room with a four-poster bed in the middle. *Okay, so this must be Clarissa's bedroom.* He gets the sense that he's alone in the room, but he doesn't know how long he's been unconscious. Anxiety grips him; the creature could return at any moment.

Standing, he immediately feels hot pain shoot up his right leg. 'Damn it!' He can barely put any pressure on it. Gritting his teeth, he takes a couple of steps. The pain is excruciating but he has no choice — he needs to find his phone and get out of here. Evie will be wondering where he is. Then a thought occurs to him: *What about Malcolm?* He hesitates momentarily, wondering what to do, then decides: *No, I can't go looking for him, it's too risky. That creature is on the loose somewhere in this house.* But his conscious pricks at him and he knows in his heart that he can't leave without him, Malcolm wouldn't leave him.

Grimacing, he tries to ignore the pain in his leg as he creeps slowly towards the door. A floorboard lets out a loud squeak and the noise sounds deafening against the silence. He stands petrified, his heart thumping in his chest. He squeezes his eyes shut, sure the creature will come hurtling through the door at any moment, but the silence drags on. Breathing a sigh of relief, he chances a few more agonising steps. He stops and listens; still nothing. Finally, he reaches the door. He puts his ear to it to check for footsteps beyond, but all he can hear is the distant rumble of thunder. He turns the door handle slowly and peers out on to the landing. Making his way over to the banister, he grips it tightly, then starts a slow and timid descent. From somewhere below he hears the unmistakable ringtone of his phone, the *Mission Impossible* theme tune.

'*Shit!*' He half hops, half falls down the rest of the stairs, almost clattering to the floor as he reaches the bottom, but he's past caring now — he has to get to his phone. It's probably Evie.

The ringing is coming from the study, its door smashed to bits. He manages to push the armchair aside and clamber over the debris of wooden splinters. He can see his phone as it vibrates gently on the carpet, the backlight torch still glowing. It stops ringing and he snatches it up. 'Oh, thank God.' He grips it tightly, turning around to check the doorway — no sign of the creature yet. He just needs to find Malcolm and get the hell out of here. His leg feeling like it's on fire as he limps across to the corner of the room.

Chapter 27
The Escape

Malcolm is trying to decide what to do. *Shall I make my way up the stairs and confront the crazy bitch? Or shall I try to find Archie first then get out through the back door in the kitchen? But who the hell is she talking to? And where is that creature?* He thinks of Archie being dragged away and a whimper escapes his lips. He can still hear Clarissa whispering when suddenly the music from the film *Mission Impossible* starts to play, making him jump.

Archie's phone! He recognises the ringtone from the care home. His mind made up, he turns and makes his way back through the little door into the study, but as he steps into the room, the ringing stops.

'Shit!' Malcolm says, as he enters the study, wondering where it landed when it fell out of Archie's hand.

'Malcolm!' Archie's voice whispers urgently.

Malcolm gasps, spinning towards the voice. 'Archie? Is that you? Oh my God, thank God you're alright! Are you alright? I can't see you properly.'

'No! It's my leg — it might be broken; you'll have to help me. We need to get out of here, we need to call the police and Evie, my daughter, as soon as possible.'

'We can go through the kitchen — there's a back door, it should be open. C'mon, I'll help you.' Malcolm moves towards Archie's voice, and after a few seconds of awkward groping, Archie finally manages to put his arm around Malcolm's neck as they make their way out of the study.

'Yeah, it's how I managed to get in,' Archie whispers, 'I knew—'

'Hang on!' Malcolm almost shrieks. 'I've just bloody realised I might have the key to the front door.' He pushes Archie up against the armchair and reaches into his back pocket pulling out the bunch of keys. He can't believe he's only just remembered he had them all this time.

'C'mon, I'll try these keys, one of them must be for the front door.'

As they make their way across the hallway, Malcolm's foot kicks something solid on the floor.

'It's the book!'

'Malcolm, leave it! Just get a move on — we need to get out now!' Archie says.

'No! I'm not leaving it here, it's proof. Hang on.' Malcolm stoops down and grabs it,

146

stuffing it under his other arm, and they hobble towards the front door.

'And *where* do you think you two are going?'

Both Malcolm and Archie spin in shock at the sound of Clarissa's voice behind them.

'Get the hell away from us, you murderer!' Malcolm yells as he starts teetering backwards towards the front door. Then, jabbing the keys at her, 'I'll... I'll poke your bloody eyes out, I swear it... Stay away from us!'

'Just let us go. Now!' shouts Archie. 'We won't say anything. Once we're out of here you can do what the hell you want, but if you come one step closer, I swear to God I'll kill you!

Clarissa lets out a gleeful laugh. 'Really, you two are hilarious. You must be the stupidest people I've ever come across. Do you honestly think a cripple and a wimp are a match for me and my beloved Herbert? I'd like to see you try. And Malcolm, dear, do you honestly think that you can just walk out of here after all the effort I put in to get you here in the first place?'

'What the hell are you talking—'

'Don't waste your breath, Malcolm — she's crazy. C'mon, we're leaving,' Archie says, backing even further towards the front door.

Malcolm passes him the bunch of keys. 'Here, you open the door. I'll keep her away,' Malcolm whispers, then holds the book aloft, ready to hit her with it.

'I'm warning you, Clarissa. Don't... don't come any nearer... I swear I will, I will really hurt you.'

'Don't worry dear, I won't have to,' she says smugly. Then, as quick as lightning, she swings her walking stick towards Malcolm and hisses. Malcolm stares in shock as the walking stick illuminates and the top of it starts to move. It's transformed into the head of some type of snake and *it* is hissing, not Clarissa.

'What the...' He stumbles into Archie, who's fumbling with the keys, trying to unlock the door. 'Argh, quick, Archie, hurry, she's got a bloody snake!'

Malcolm stares dumbfounded at the walking stick, which has now transformed into a writhing serpent and is standing upright beside Clarissa, about six feet tall. As they start gliding forward as one, the serpent bares its fangs and lunges at him.

Screaming, Malcolm flings the book at it as he dives to the side. The serpent narrowly misses him but hits Archie in the back. The keys skitter across the floor and Archie crumples to the ground in a heap.

Malcolm runs towards the kitchen but he can't leave Archie. Turning, he shouts, 'Archie, get up, run!'

The serpent's head is glowing, so Malcolm can see exactly what it's doing, despite the darkness. It's repeatedly lunging at Archie as he scuttles across the floor on his backside, crying out with each strike.

I must do something! Malcolm thinks desperately.

His entire body shaking, Malcolm slowly starts to move towards Archie. He can see Clarissa in his peripheral vision as she looks on, whispering to the serpent in some unknown language.

Good, she's distracted. He sweeps his foot across the floor from side to side until finally it makes contact with the book. Bending down very slowly, so he doesn't catch the serpent's attention, he picks it up, then takes the lighter out of his back pocket. He flicks the lighter on and holds it near to the corner of the book.

'Call your bloody snake off or I'll burn your precious book and this house down with it — right now!' Malcolm yells at Clarissa.

Clarissa and the serpent turn as one towards him.

'Malcolm dear, now don't be silly, put the book down,' she says tightly. 'You shouldn't play with things you don't understand.'

'You're deranged! Do you honestly think you'll get away with this?' Malcolm shouts back.

'Malcolm, we have been getting away with this for hundreds of years! My dear boy, you really are naïve aren't you, eh?' she says, laughing. 'Do you honestly think my Herbert will let you escape?'

'That's another thing!' he shouts, 'I don't believe you! You probably killed him too, you mad bitch! I bet... I bet you don't even have a husband! You probably got that — that bloody creature to kill him!' he spits at her.

'Oh Malcolm, it's so kind of you to concern yourself with his welfare, but I can assure you Herbert is alive and well... In fact, he's right here with us.'

She turns towards the serpent and whispers something.

Malcolm stops breathing as he witnesses the serpent transform before his eyes into the tall white creature that chased and attacked Archie. Suddenly it feels like a vice has gripped his chest. He clutches at his heart as he gasps for breath, but no air seems to be reaching his lungs.

I can't let that thing kill us. A picture of his mum waiting for him flashes through his mind.

He flicks the lighter on and touches the corner of the book to the flame. It catches alight immediately, and he has to turn it quickly in his hands so it doesn't burn his fingers. The flame flares up the spine of the book and he hurls it through the open door of the study.

'No!' Clarissa screams as she runs towards the study, arms outstretched. The creature, Herbert, tilts his head and starts wailing, then chases after Clarissa.

Malcolm can see the book has landed on the armchair, setting it alight too.

Quickly he turns towards the heap on the floor. 'Archie, Archie! C'mon, we haven't got long.' He stoops over Archie's shattered body. 'Please, Archie, wake up!'

Archie groans incoherently as Malcolm grabs his arm and shakes him. *It's no use, I'll have to drag him.* Putting his hands under Archie's armpits, he starts to haul him towards the kitchen door, pure primal fear driving him on.

Sweat trickles into his eyes as he continues to heave Archie's weighty body with him toward the kitchen. Finally, his back hits the kitchen door. He turns to open it, then resumes dragging Archie through the kitchen towards to the back door on the other side of the room. He pulls down on the handle but it's locked.

'Fuck! No, no, no! I don't believe it!' His mind racing, he knows the kitchen window is stuck solid and the keys to the door are somewhere in the hall. He can't face going back out there to look for them. His eyes dart around the room for anything that he can smash the window with but there's absolutely nothing.

'Okay, Archie, listen, I have to go back and find the keys. Whatever you do, don't make a sound.' Taking a deep breath, and with nothing but thoughts of getting out of this hellhole, he creeps over to the door. As soon as he opens it, he hears loud crackling as flames billow out of the study, lighting up the hallway. Scanning the floor as he walks towards the front door, he hopes they are both burning to death in there. Feeling the intense heat on his face, he sees the keys lying on one of the white tiles just ahead of him. He picks them up then bolts straight back to the kitchen, but just as he's pushing the door open, something sharp stabs him in the back.

'Argh!' Malcolm screams as his head hits the door with the force of the blow. Turning, he sees the serpent a couple of feet in front of him. Its snakelike body is on fire and it's writhing and screaming in agony. Then it pulls its head back, baring its fangs, and makes to strike for Malcolm's face.

Malcolm raises his arms instinctively to protect his face but loses his footing and goes tumbling backwards through the kitchen door. Scrambling to his knees, he slams the door shut, just in time to hear the serpents fangs hit the other side of the door.

Swiping the sweat off his face with his coat sleeve, he runs to the back door and sticks the first key in. It's the wrong one. He tries the next one, but his hands are shaking so badly that he struggles to get it in the lock. Eventually it turns. He gives it a hard twist and he hears the door unlock. 'Thank God!'

As he pulls the door open wide, the wind immediately hits him in the face, almost taking his breath away. He leaves it swinging wildly as he runs over to Archie, who's slumped on the floor where he left him. 'C'mon— we're nearly there. Can you hear me? Archie? Archie?'

Archie doesn't respond.

Malcolm puts his hands under Archie's armpits but it's no good, he's a dead weight. He takes hold of his ankles instead, and huffing and puffing, he pulls him towards the back door.

'I'm sorry, but it's the only way.'

Archie lets out a low groan as Malcolm slides him across the floor. Eventually they reach the doorstep, and as a surge of adrenalin courses through Malcolm's body, he manages to heave Archie over the threshold and outside into the driving rain.

Chapter 28
The Aftermath

Malcolm can hear the distant sound of fire engines as rain pelts his face. Overwhelmed with relief that he managed to get them both out of the house alive, he looks over at Archie, who's sprawled out on the garden path, getting soaked.

'You okay?' Malcom says, leaning over, hand outstretched to help him up.

'Um, I need my phone. I've got to call Evie,' says Archie.

Archie is covered in blood and the rain is making it run down his face into his clothes.

'You need to get to hospital! We need to call an ambulance.'

Archie yelps in pain as Malcolm helps him stand. Holding Malcolm for support, he takes his phone out of his pocket.

Malcolm hears the sirens drawing closer. 'What do you want to do? Shall we wait for them to get here? We'll have to explain everything. What if they don't believe us?'

'I've no bloody intention of staying here, no. C'mon, we're getting out of here before they arrive. Help me over to that back gate, it's how I got into the house. There's an alleyway that runs down the side of the house and leads to the road. My car's parked up there.'

Malcolm supports Archie as they hobble over to the gate and he opens the latch.

'It's this way,' Archie says, nodding his head to the left as he brings the phone up to his ear.

'Dad, where the hell are you? What's happened — I've been calling you for ages!'

Malcolm can hear a young female voice yelling through the phone.

'Evie love, listen carefully, I don't want you to panic, I'm fine, but I had a bit of an accident. You're going to have to stay over at Melanie's house tonight, okay?'

'What? Oh my God, Dad, are you okay? What... what happened? Did you crash the car?'

Malcolm can hear the panic in the voice on the phone as they continue to hobble down the dark alleyway towards the road.

'Um, yes, that's it, love. I just had a slight accident but honestly I'm okay and the car's fine. Don't worry, I promise I'm alright. I'll make my own way home, but please just text me when you've spoken to Melanie's mum and she says it okay for you to stay over, okay?'

'Yep, okay Dad, I promise I will. Love you.'

Malcolm thinks about asking Archie if he can call his mum, but thinks better of it. She'd only worry, and besides, he just wants to get home.

'So, do you think you're alright to drive?' asks Malcolm.

'Gonna have to be,' Archie says. 'I'll drop you off, then I'll go straight home and take a look at these cuts.'

They both fall into silence as the sheer horror of the night only now starts to sink in. Malcolm is suddenly aware of the acute pain on his back where the serpent's fangs bit into his flesh. He'll wait until he's at home to check it.

The light from the streetlamp comes in to view as they reach the bottom of the alleyway. They turn to look at the house, staring at the inferno. Flames are licking through all the window frames now, and the glass is all but gone. Black smoke billows outwards like noxious vomit, then gets eaten up by the wind and rain.

Malcolm turns to Archie.

'Um… So, what… what exactly do you think they were? Do you think they're dead?'

Archie drops his arm from Malcolm's shoulder and shrugs. 'I don't know. As for being dead? I fucking hope so,' he whispers. 'C'mon, there's my car.'

As they drive away from the curb, three fire engines come racing up the road, lights flashing and sirens blaring, coming to a stop outside the burning Manse.

Archie and Malcolm look at each other. No words are needed.

'Let's get you home, and by the way, that coat looks terrible on you.' Archie says as he puts the car into gear.

Epilogue

A week later, Malcolm and his mum are celebrating that in just one weeks' time they'll be travelling to Ireland. They're sat in their tiny kitchen, having just finished eating a takeaway. Malcolm starts clearing the dirty plates away, but as he stands to put them in the sink, he starts to feel queasy again. It's been happening a lot since he got home. He dumps them clumsily on the draining board and clutches his stomach as it rumbles loudly.

'You okay, love? You look a bit pale,' his mum says, looking concerned.

'Yeah, I'm okay, Mum — just got a dicky tummy is all. C'mon, let's watch some TV, shall we?'

As Malcolm settles his mum into her armchair, the need to open his bowels becomes urgent, and he has a sudden overwhelming urge to throw up. Bile starts to rise in his throat and he thrusts the TV remote control at her.

'Here, Mum. You put the telly on, I'm just nipping to the loo.' Almost gagging now, with his hand covering his mouth, he bolts upstairs to the bathroom.

What a waste of money, he thinks as he pulls the chain for the third time. His belly muscles feel sore from all the heaving. Finally, whatever has made him feel ill is out of his system — he hopes.

He runs the tap in the bathroom sink, cupping his hand to rinse the foul taste from his mouth. As he's bent over, thinking he should really use mouthwash, or better still, brush his teeth, an ice-cold sensation starts crawling up his body. It's such a bizarre feeling, he's sure he must be imagining it. It rises slowly up through his body from his feet. With the tap still running, he pauses mid-slosh, waiting for the sensation to stop, but it doesn't — it continues up through the back of his legs, the middle of his torso, all the way up his neck, then out through the top of his head. Then it's gone, and he suddenly feels very light. *Weird. I must be coming down with something. Hardly surprising really, after what I've been through.*

'Are you alright, love? What's the matter?' his mum calls up the stairs.

He can only just hear her reedy voice over the running water. Then he hears another voice. It must be Natalie, the carer. She has a key and normally lets herself in. He remembers then that she's come to administer his mum's medications.

He grips the edge of the sink and slowly straightens up, mentally assessing the feeling in each part of his body to check the effects of the strange numbness. He wiggles his ankle, then lifts his leg — everything seems to feel okay. Standing, he looks at his reflection in the mirror.

He gasps, his mouth dropping open as he stares in horror at the face staring back at him. His dark beady eyes are now silver pinpricks. His face has turned parchment white, his cheekbones protruding grotesquely from the rest of his face, reminding him of two sunken tombstones in a decaying bed of ashen silt. He tries to scream but all that escapes from his mouth is a low guttural sound that descends into a small, defeated whimper. He continues to stare at the alien face reflected back at him, transfixed with terror. He opens and closes his mouth slowly. The black pointed teeth that lie within look sharp and shiny in the over-bright light. He moves his head from side to side, slowly at first, then quickly — trying to catch the reflection out in its lie. *This has to be some sort of weird hallucination.* But the reflection mimics his every move perfectly. Something originating from the back of his throat is tickling the inside of his new black shiny teeth. He opens his mouth to let whatever it is out, then stares mesmerised as a black forked tongue whips lasciviously over his lips.

His reflection smiles.

Pulling the corded light switch, he turns out of the bathroom and down the stairs, calling to his mum.

'Was that Natalie I heard at the door, Mum? I hope so — I'm absolutely starving.'

Acknowledgements

The biggest thank you to my daughter Lauren and my sister Belinda, my true angels. I couldn't have written this book without your unwavering love, support and encouragement.

Thank you to my husband Steve and my brother Clive for their early feedback.

And last but not least, thank you to my parents for the legacy they left me - their everlasting love. I miss them always, but they've been with me every step of the way.

Printed in Great Britain
by Amazon

46725748R00098